The DOWNSIZING of HUDSON FOSTER

A NOVEL

Harlin Hailey

TO MY FATHER

There is no such thing as a free lunch.
-An old American adage

-1-

EVERY SO OFTEN somebody's gotta come along and rock the boat. That'd be me. My name is Hudson Foster. I promise I'll keep my story short because I know in the visual Information Age you for sure got other shit to do. So I swear to God, I won't keep you long. Just long enough to tell it like it is.

I'm not gonna lie to you either. This ain't one of them suddenly-she-turned stories, or one of them *"I'll be back"* cornball thrillers where some foreign beefcake blows some other clown out of his shoes with a rocket launcher. It's definitely not that. We already have enough of that crap at the movies. So if you don't want to learn something about the real world, then haul ass. 'Cause I don't have time for dummies—don't have time to dish pearls to swine. But don't get scared. I'm not feeding you *Ivanhoe* here. It's a fairly easy read. And who knows? I might even make you laugh. Mixing humor with profundity is what I do best, you know. I just happen to be in a pickle right now. I'm unemployed. So forgive me if I go off on you. I don't mean to hurt your feelings. But somebody's got to give it to you straight. Somebody other than a spin doctor. Somebody other than your favorite pop star. You might not always agree with what I have to say. But that's okay. It means you've got a brain. And it means I've done my job. Because that's what I'm all about, I guess … checks and balances. Making sure you—whoever the hell you are—don't get screwed.

But please, don't confuse me with one of those "questing guy" or coming-of-age stories, because I've never really searched for the meaning of life. Nor do I intend to. So I'm not here to whine or give you excuses. I'm here to give you answers. Answers that will stand the test of time. Answers that I learned the hard way after I got downsized from my job.

I guess that's what my story's all about, really. Searching for a job and finding something much more. Bro Rich—you'll meet him later—wanted me to do a screenplay on my adventures in interview-land. He said that's where the dough is. But I told him that a film wasn't the proper forum for what I had to say. Screenplays don't ever tell you nothin' you don't already know. Sure, they make you the big dough if they sell, but I'm not in it for the money. Not yet, anyway.

Call me stupid for trying to help out the next guy. Everybody else does. They say, "Hudson, what's your motivation, man? Why the selfless crusade to help other people you don't even know?"

And then I say, "That's exactly what's wrong with the world today. Everybody's got an angle, a goal to reach." Well, I'm here to tell you sometimes people just do things because they care. It's as simple as that.

But don't get me wrong. I ain't no psalm-singing-holier-than-thou-virtue-vulture if that's what you think. Nor am I a zealot. A brazen and didactic wild man, maybe, but not a zealot. I don't represent any particular political philosophy, and I'm sure as hell not going to try to convert you to one of those incense-burning Eastern religions. (I'm allergic to the smelly smoke.)

No, I'm just here to give you some helpful insights into the new millennium. Hints from Heloise. That kind of shit. Hints you can use as you search for your unique niche in this crazy life. If you want, you can think of me as your wake-up call. Not an alarm clock, but a sledgehammer. And if you want to listen, then that's cool. If you don't, well, that's cool too. Just keep one thing in mind. This book's the only place you're gonna get this kinda inside information. Socrates is dead.

And there ain't no CliffsNotes.

One more thing. Please excuse my cussing and lousy grammar, and my informal way of addressing things sometimes. I've never written a book before, so I might sound like some tough street kid one minute and some erudite nimrod the next. I guess it just goes with the turf when you're suddenly stripped of your identity. But I'll eventually find my rhythm, so bear with me. The last thing I need is some damn armchair editor telling me I've got some kind of a character conflict going on … duh.

Anyhow, I'm ready to begin my story now, so if you want to get up and go, you can. I'm not stopping you. Nobody wants to listen anymore anyway. Much less open a book. But if you're committed to the truth, then you owe it to yourself to read on. If not, you can be a sucker for the rest of your life.

It's up to you.

-2-

IT ALL STARTED on my twenty-ninth birthday. It was a Monday, November 23. The same year Sinatra died, Clinton was impeached, and Mark "Big Mac" McGwire slugged seventy home runs. I remember being suddenly awakened that morning at 6:30 a.m. by the slap and patter of rain against my apartment window. It was the second storm of the season in Los Angeles, but it wasn't a cold one. We had El Niño to blame for that. (Of course, we blamed everything on El Niño that year, including bizarre behavior.)

I remember feeling good that morning. It being my birthday, I was looking forward to going into the office and having cake with my coworkers, and then reading all the insincere but humorous comments they had been forced to write inside my birthday card.

You know the cracks I'm talking about. Things like, "You're a real stand-up guy, Hudson. Happy B-day." Or, better yet, "Thank you for being such a good friend." (This comment was almost always written by some kiss-ass you'd known less than a week.) Then of course there would be the usual old man remarks, diaper quips and Geritol jokes. The standard over-the-hill humor we all have to endure once we hit that age.

But of all my birthday perks, I was most looking forward to sneaking a glass or two of champagne with the new girl from marketing. Her name was Helen, and she was a recent Rutgers University graduate. As practically everyone knows, Rutgers is borderline Ivy League.

I was eight years older than Helen, but she had already given me the impression that she liked older dudes. We had talked often, swapped astrological signs and birthdays (which apparently were quite compatible), and gotten into the exhilarating habit of touching the other's arm while laughing at each other's jokes. But nothing more than this office foreplay had occurred on the sexual front. However, I must confess to you now, on that day my thoughts were definitely centered below the belt. Leave it to a birthday to invigorate the old libido.

I took my time getting dressed that morning. Made sure I looked my best. I meticulously polished up my nicest pair of cordovan wingtips, put on a red silk tie, then slipped on the closer … a nine-hundred-dollar, dove-gray pinstripe suit. It was—I had been readily assured by the salesman—a real "chick killer."

I looked in the mirror and smiled. I felt like Philip Marlowe calling on four million dollars.

"Let's rock," I told my reflection.

When I got to the bank that morning, everything seemed normal.

The tellers all greeted me with their usual money-counting smiles. The listless new accounts people nodded at me the way they always did: purse-lipped and tight, like Scrooge poring over his parchment ledgers. It was a jealous greeting, I knew, pathetic and childish, but it was something that I had grown accustomed to in a perverted sort of way.

Later on, I would come to find out that this type of animosity between slothful, low-salaried employees and successful, salary-plus-commission employees exists in almost all American corporations.

That's just the way it is. Envy and jealousy will always be cozy bedfellows with capitalism.

I guess—before I go any further—I should probably tell you a little bit about my former career and myself. That will help you understand the horrors that lie ahead. I won't tell you where I went to college though, only to say that it was in California and my major was business. I don't want my college professors reading this book and thinking it was all their fault that I turned out the way I did. All those old schools are so steeped in rosy history and tradition that sometimes they lose sight of the real world. You can't blame them, though. Every school wants its alumni to do well, especially since they'll be hitting them up for cash for the rest of their natural lives.

Maybe if I'd been a better student, then *maybe* I might have told you the name of the school. But my transcripts were nothing special. All right, they stunk. But you know what? I learned just as much about life outside of the classroom as I did inside. I know grades are important, but hey, they're definitely not everything. I guess the key is balance. Something I'm still learning today.

I socialized my way through most of the eighties. I skipped class a lot and experimented with that whole *Less Than Zero* thing. But it wasn't like I was addicted to drugs or alcohol. I never tried anything heavy. Never got a tattoo. And I wasn't one of those angst-ridden youths the press wanted me to be. (Groups are easier to market to.)

In fact, it was quite the opposite. I was just having fun—on Daddy's money of course—chasing girls, jamming to the sounds of heavy metal, and letting the winds of hedonism blow me in any direction they pleased. I guess you could say I was livin' large. No worries. No responsibilities. I thought I owned the world back then. That money grew on trees. That futures and careers were mine to be chosen and controlled. I was absolutely, positively, carved-in-stone sure that making a million bucks was my God-given right. That was my problem. I thought I was special.

It's funny how certain you can be of things when you're young. That nothing bad can ever happen to you. That old people don't know shit and should get the bloody hell out of the way and let youth rule. Looking back on it, I know now I couldn't have been more wrong. The lessons of immortality are—I have finally come to understand—rarely introduced before the age of twenty-five.

When I finally did graduate (it took me five years), I got a job at this small bank in Westwood, shipping mortgage loans. Really all I did was stuff semi-important documents into a brown folder and give them to this suave, drunk guy in secondary marketing to sell to some other bank for a lot of money.

Several times, I watched him usher this blonde secretary into his office, close the door, and come out an hour later with a crooked grin on his face. It happened so often I can still picture it. She'd always emerge looking real serious and shit, holding files close to her big boobs and nodding like she was really gung ho about the bottom line.

But you could tell that she'd just been bent over some antique credenza. It was so obvious. Her cheeks were all pink and flushed, and she kept unsuccessfully trying to blow a loose strand of blonde hair off her face as her boss/lover stood in his office door barking out hollow-ringing instructions on some mundane business matter.

"That'll be all for today, Ms. Abernathy," he'd say. "Please, remember what I said, and keep me posted on that Union Federal deal."

"Yes, sir," she'd answer, a look of fraudulent determination on her face. "Right away, sir."

I have to admit there were moments when I fantasized about

somehow wrangling my way into that guy's job. But the bank was suddenly bought out a few months later by an East Coast insurance firm, and the entire staff was laid off. Including me. I wasn't too depressed about it though. I was only twenty-three years old at the time, and the whole world was still my oyster. Little did I know that the tide of American business was starting to change.

And change fast.

It didn't take me long to find another job. As the saying goes, youth will be served. Only a week in fact. And it was a good job, too. Much better pay, and better-tasting coffee. Frontier Savings and Loan. "New Visions for a New World." That is our slogan. Or was. They're out of business now, too. Bought out by another East Coast firm looking to swallow the "New West."

That merger—as you might already have guessed—was the inspiration behind this story. I had given Frontier Savings and Loan five and a half years of my life. Given them my blood, sweat, and tears. I had risen to the position of assistant vice president and was being groomed for even bigger things. That's what they told me anyway. And I believed them.

Each year I had gotten a raise, and each year my responsibilities had increased. I was handling new accounts, originating home loans, and creating and implementing marketing programs for the bank's new financial products. I know it sounds geeky, but I was a serious businessman now, making forty-eight grand a year, eating big salads, and wearing sober blue suits.

I had even stepped up from driving my Honda Accord to motoring about L.A. in a new BMW—light blue with a palomino interior. I was totally focused, climbing the corporate ladder with such fearless intensity that I had failed to notice what was happening all around me. (Not unlike an about-to-be-ambushed contestant on *The Jerry Springer Show*.)

When the recession hit in the early nineties—and the real estate market dived—the bank went through a restructuring period. Mass firings. People I knew dropping like flies. Slashing the payroll was the classic way for corporations to generate short-term profits back then, thus pacifying their shareholders. It was typical American know-how at its best. Putting money before people.

I felt bad because all these old dudes over forty with kids in college and big mortgages were getting the ax and shit, laid off without warning. And these were all guys who had been with the company for over twenty years! I kept telling myself, "That's never going to happen to me." I rationalized that the guys who'd been laid off were nothing but a bunch of losers, a defeated bunch of Dilberts. All you had to do was look at them trudging out of the building one by one, with their boxes of stuff held against their soft, bulging bellies, rulers and pencils sticking out of their back pockets like prison shanks.

After witnessing the carnage that sad afternoon, I promised myself I'd never carry a box out if I got fired. Never. I'd leave all my junk in there if I had to. I wasn't going to give anybody the satisfaction of seeing ole Hudson Foster walk the line. No siree. I got my pride. That's why I don't decorate my workspace anymore. Doesn't pay to get comfortable anywhere but home.

Anyhow, after the dust had finally settled—and the bank showed a slim profit because of the layoffs—everyone started to feel good again. The president of the company, Mr. Prichard, kept telling me that I was the future of Frontier Savings and Loan now. That, with vision, I could do anything. One day he stopped me in the hallway and held out an acorn in the palm of his hand and said, "Hudson, what do you see in this acorn?" He shoved it closer to my face.

"I see a tree," I said, knowing that the old man was fond of posing intelligent riddles. "A tree so big and thick and green that it could shade the entire city of Los Angeles."

He smiled. "That's good, son. But it's not the right answer."

"Then what is?" I asked, puzzled.

He stared at the acorn like it was an oracle. "When I see this acorn, I see a forest. A forest so dense and lush that it could shade the entire world. Now that, Mr. Foster, *is vision*."

Deep, I remember thinking. Real deep. Which reminds me. I might as well give you your first tip while I'm thinking about it. Everybody nowadays is always throwing that word *vision* around like they really know what it means. It's a bunch of horseshit, really. Fodder for the advertising cannon. No company ever lives up to their promises anymore, especially the ones that have the word *vision* in their corporate slogan. So if you see *that* word in some company's advertising, run like hell. You'll be better off, I promise.

Now that you know a little bit about me—and my former career at Frontier—I guess it's time to get back to my birthday. The infamous day it all happened. Oh, just one other thing. You're probably wondering what I look like, so I might as well get that over with too. I'm six feet tall—give or take half an inch—with fence-brown hair and earth-green eyes. If I had to rate myself on the attractiveness scale, I'd say I was about a six, maybe a weak seven on a good day. People are always telling me I remind them of somebody when they first meet me, but they never seem to be sure who the other person is. I don't know if that's good or bad. I guess I've just got one of those faces that blends in well in a crowd. I am—I have come to realize—the poster boy for the common man.

Anyway, when I got to my desk that morning, I found a couple of balloons tied around my phone and some roses in a glass vase. Just then a couple of the female tellers yelled at me in gleeful unison, "Happy birthday, Hudson."

"Thank you," I said, pulling off my beige trench coat and placing it casually over my chair. My desk—along with those of the half-dozen other assistant vice presidents—was located on the bank's main floor and, looking around, I noticed that Mr. Decker, the bank's manager, was away from his desk. I thought little of his absence, for it was highly likely that he was in another department crunching the bank's most recent numbers.

My eyes fell on Bernie, the rotund mutual funds guy at the desk next to mine. He seemed oblivious to my birthday celebration. He was reading the *Wall Street Journal* with his feet propped up on the desk and his mouth full of blueberry muffin. Now there was a real picture of vision for ya.

"How you doing today, Bernie?" I asked.

"Lousy," he mumbled through the muffin. "My stocks are tankin'. Can you believe it? An eight-year bull market and I gotta pick the only technology stocks that go down."

I laughed inside. I secretly wished the fat oaf would lose his shirt. Not only was he overweight and obnoxious, he was also dishonest. He was fond of churning customers' accounts without their knowledge, a practice I abhorred. But of all his glaring faults, it was his gross habit of picking his butt when he stood up from his desk that irked me the most. Especially the times he did it when I had a client at my desk.

I said, "Cheer up, ole buddy. I'm sure come nine o'clock some blue-haired old lady will totter in the door with a coupla hundred grand, looking for you to make her financial dreams come true."

"Let's hope so," he said, without looking up from his paper. "Just one naive old bag a day keeps the Bern man in the chips."

"You're a real gem, Bernie," I said. "Don't ever change."

He laughed out loud, prompting half the floor to hiss,

"Ssshhh!" Bernie was about as popular among the bank staff as the last team of auditors.

I sat down at my desk and read the card on the roses and smiled. It was from Helen. It said, "Happy Birthday. Hope your day is filled with joy and love. P.S. Don't forget about our twelve o'clock lunch. See you then. Love, Helen." I felt my penis twitch with excitement. Then suddenly—just as my lustful fantasies were about to rocket to new heights—the goddamn phone rang. My manhood shriveled.

"This is Hudson," I answered.

"Hudson, Rick Decker."

It was my boss. "Yeah, Rick," I said, as exuberantly as I could manage under the circumstances. "Good morning. What's up?"

"Got a minute?"

A wave of panic rushed through me. Any time a boss ever starts a conversation with *Got a minute?* you need to worry. It's the universal opening among hatchet men.

"Yeah, sure, Rick," I said. "You want to meet here, or should I come see you?"

"Neither," he said. "Prichard's office. Two minutes."

"Yeah, all right," I said, my mouth suddenly dry. "I'll see you up there … bye."

I hung up the phone and took a deep breath. That's when it hit me. The birthday greetings from my coworkers had been a ruse. A clever charade to dull my instincts. I was about to get the old meet-me-in-the-office routine. Not a goddamn cake-and-cookie affair. I began to panic. But only for a moment. Then a calming sense of inevitability took over. If the bastards can me, so what? I'm still young. I can get another job. I mean, I got skills—right?

I let my body muscles relax for a second. Then I rode the elevator to the fourth floor and tiptoed out. The bland hallway, usually shoulder to shoulder with shirt-sleeved executives scurrying about, was eerily silent and deserted this morning. What was going on? I thought. The answer was suddenly there in my head. What a fool I'd been. I hadn't been summoned up here to be axed. Prichard—that lovable old bastard—was obviously throwing me a surprise party!

All the guys on that floor—all those people who worked behind the closed doors I was passing—were probably hiding in the boss's office, just waiting to jump out and blow those funny tickler things that give off a shrill whistle when they unwind. I began to get a warm feeling inside. To think that they would go to all this trouble for a knucklehead like me.

I can't tell you the sheer exhilaration I felt at that moment. I realize now, of course, that my boundless joy made me—how shall I put it?—incautious. Crazy is probably closer.

Given that frame of mind, I think what I did next is understandable. At least in retrospect. So here goes. I barged right into Prichard's office unannounced—my eyes closed and my arms spread out like some over-the-top opera singer—and I scream-sing at the top of my freakin' lungs, "SURPRISE!"

In the long, breathless moment that followed, I heard no shouts of returned joy. Only a lone male voice that sounded as flat and annoying as a busy signal. "Yes, I guess you could call it that. Please have a seat, Mr. Foster."

I opened my eyes … and gasped. There was no horde of deliriously happy celebrants in the room. Only a man I'd never seen before, sitting behind Prichard's desk. I guessed him to be about sixty-five years old, with short silver hair, hollow black eyes, and high, sharp cheekbones. His suit—a hand-tailored corporate-raider blue number—screamed power.

"I won't bite, son," he said, his pointy teeth sparkling in the light when he smiled. "I promise."

"Who are you?" I said, my eyes frantically searching the richly appointed office. "And what have you done with Mr. Prichard?"

"Mr. Prichard is no longer with the firm," he said. He motioned toward a chair in front of his polished desk. "Please have a seat, Mr. Foster."

I approached cautiously and sat down. The man before me was a predator. No doubt about that. He reminded me of an NFL team owner, a win-at-all-costs look haunting his bony old face.

On his desk—it was *his* desk now, you could tell by how comfortable he looked—I noticed a jade crocodile and two crystal shark sculptures. A far cry from Mr. Prichard's old decor: two pictures of his lumpy wife and a framed quote from Ben Franklin, "A penny saved is a penny earned."

"What's going on here?" I said, glancing nervously at a bunch of empty boxes stacked near the rear wall of the wood-paneled room.

He leaned forward and smiled, his canines glistening. "What's going on here, Mr. Foster, is a corporate cleansing. It's out with the dolphins and in with the sharks. In short, Frontier has been bought out by another firm in a hostile takeover. Which means—"

"Which means what?" I said.

He leaned back and crossed his arms and regarded me with a look of infinite patience. "They said you were a powder keg. But then, I like feisty. Do you know what day it is?"

"Yeah," I said. "It's my birthday. So you'd better show me a cake, preferably German chocolate, or I'm gonna get ugly right here on the dance floor."

His face soured. "It looks like you're a man who prefers to take his lumps the old-fashioned way, Mr. Foster. So I'll give it to you straight. *You're fired.* You see those boxes over there? Pick one and get the hell out of my office!"

He flipped a cellophane-windowed envelope across the desk, and it flew into my lap. I tore it open and found a check for three thousand dollars made out to me. Along with a termination slip. Pink, just like they always said it would be. I felt the rage welling up inside. I couldn't believe this was happening to me. ME! Hudson Foster, the perfect corporate creation. Not here. Not like this. NOT A BOX!

"I want your belongings packed up in fifteen minutes," he said without emotion, "and you out of the building five minutes after that."

"That's it?" I said. "I give this firm six years of my life, and all I get is three grand and an empty box from a man with no name?"

"Think of yourself as a free agent, Mr. Foster. Not unemployed. It's better that way. I believe the proper terminology nowadays is *between opportunities*." A thin smile crossed his arrogant face. "Now please hurry along. Others are waiting to get on the ride."

Like a zombie, I got up slowly and walked over and picked out a box. I felt like Charlie Brown on Halloween. *I got a rock.*

"Please let me know if you need a recommendation," he said. "I pride myself on writing ringing references."

I walked over to his desk, holding my empty box out in front of me like a pregnant woman grasping her belly. I was ready to explode. My lips were quivering and my heart was racing. "I'll pass on the ringing reference," I said, tight-lipped. "But there is something else you can do for me."

"Name it."

I lifted the cardboard container and shouted, "You can bend over while I stuff this box up your ass!"

That got his attention. The old axman panicked and smashed a thumb down on the intercom button. "Security!"

"Oh, great!" I said, tossing the box to one side and flouncing my arms in disgust. "That's just great. Calling security." I leaned over his desk and grabbed his stapler. "How would you like it if I staple-gunned your ass cheeks together, huh? Would you like that? C'mon! Just give me the word. 'Cause I'll do it. I'm ready."

I strode across the room in a rage and kicked the boxes against the wall, then heaved the stapler. "You don't even know who I am, you asshole! How many other lives do you plan to ruin before lunch? Huh? Answer me that, Shark Man!"

He didn't get the chance to, because two gnarly security guards barged in and grabbed me by the arms. As they held me immobile before his desk, the old hatchet man leaned forward and stared at me hard.

"This concludes your exit interview with Frontier, Mr. Foster. And since you have demonstrated marked hostility toward the bank and toward me personally, you will be escorted out of the building and *watched* until you have driven safely out of the parking lot. Your things will be shipped to you overnight via UPS." He eyed the guards and waved his right hand in disgust. "Now get him the hell out of here."

"One sick day!" I shouted as they were dragging me backward. "Only one goddamn sick day in my entire stay at Frontier. And you want to know somethin' funny, Shark Man? I wasn't even sick. I was hungover!" I laughed hysterically. "I got wasted the night before on five shots of Jägermeister. I was fried. You hear that? Fried on company time! How does that grab you, asshole?"

My body was suddenly jerked through the open doorway and out into the hall. The door slammed shut behind me—the sound of rejection echoing loudly down the wide corridor as the two corporate goons dragged me toward the elevator.

I gotta tell ya, it was one helluva way to start my birthday.

-3-

I NEVER GOT a chance to say goodbye to Helen. Shark Man had
seen to that. The bastard. I guess I could've called her at the office,
but I didn't. I was too damned embarrassed about losing my job,
and I felt like half a man. Besides, starting a relationship out of
sheer desperation never seems to work. People smell fear, and they
usually don't dig it. I knew I had to let her go. She might have
been one of the few who had boldly leaned their heads out of their
office doors that day, discreetly whispering promises to keep in
touch as the burly guards whisked me out of the building. But I
don't remember her. Everything was blurry and slow, like an
accident in progress. I can still hear those hallway whispers in my
head, though.

 —*Hey, Hudson, don't worry about it, man. My brother's starting
a new company on the Net. E-commerce and sporting goods. It'll make
us all rich. I'll call you.*

 —*Hudson, sweetie, I know it seems like rotten timing, but it's
actually a blessing in disguise. Trust me. I'm this close to funding my
new film company. I could use a good creative man like you.*

 —*Pssst, Hudson, buddy. I got a couple of moonlighting gigs
happening—phone cards. Cat condos. Easy sell. I'll hook you up.*

All bullshit. I'm telling you that right now. I never heard from any of those people again. And you won't either. Because the first rule of being fired is to never believe anything a coworker tells you after the fact. Oh, they might mean well, because they're only human after all, but trust me, they're all too afraid of losing their own jobs to help out the next guy. Especially a fallen comrade. Nobody wants to be seen cavorting with the enemy. Besides, every one of them is working on some entrepreneurial venture that never seems to pan out. It's an American tradition. So just be aware of all the hollow promises that you'll receive while you're gathering up your things and packing them angrily into your little brown box. Because that's all they are, hollow promises.

I learned a couple of other things on that day, too. One is if management is always calling meetings to tell you how secure your job is, then you're definitely in danger of losing your job. That's just the way it is. Just once, I wish they would come clean with you and tell you the truth. *"Hey, people, we're in deep guano here."* But they don't. They send in some "understanding" bald man with a bow tie and happy crinkles around his eyes to sugarcoat lies to you until the day the hatchet man arrives. It certainly isn't fair. So don't think that it is. But I guess the most important thing that I would like to impart to you about the day I got fired is try to keep a cool head when they can you. You never know when you might cross paths with some of those people again. I know it sounds crazy, because the last people you ever want to see again are the people who changed your life for the worst, but trust me, the karmic wheel spins in mysterious ways. I wish I would've kept my cool, but I couldn't help it. I guess I'm just a passionate guy by nature. Helen told me that I did crazy impulsive things sometimes because I was a Sagittarius. Always firing my arrows without looking where they were landing. I'm not much for astrology, but I have to admit that the adjectives used to describe Sagittarius kinda fit me: honest, generous, philosophical, idealistic, foolhardy with reckless abandon. I agree with honest and generous, but foolhardy and reckless abandon are two traits I'm still grappling with. I still go ballistic—more to come—but I'm getting better about controlling my emotions.

Anyhow, the first thing I did when I got home that day was grab my checkbook. Other people will tell you stories about how they got fired and how the first thing they did when they got home was get stinking drunk. But not me. The first thing I did was pull out my checkbook and scan my bank balance. Then I got stinking drunk. Including the three grand that I had just received as a parting gift from my former employer, I had a total sum of thirty-two hundred dollars in my account. I started to sweat. That would cover December's bills and January's rent, but little else. That meant only one thing … a holiday job search.

"Ho ho ho" quickly became "Dough dough dough."

I wished now that I hadn't sunk all my money into that BMW. Damn car. But after a few see-through cocktails, my confidence started to return, and I remember thinking that finding another job would be just as easy as the last time.

Boy, was I wrong.

-4-

IT DIDN'T TAKE long for the panic to set in. Two hours later, my baby sister, Hillary, called from Vermont. She was out of breath and talking fast. "Hudson, it's me. I need your help. It's snowing bad and the car conked out, and Dad won't pay for it. So please call me when you get this message. Oh yeah, happy birth—"

"Hold on, Hill," I said softly. "Slow down."

"Oh, my God!" she said, surprised. "It's you. I thought I was talking to a machine."

"No, it's me in the flesh," I said.

She paused, then asked the question carefully. "Aren't you supposed to be at work?"

"One would think so on a Monday at two in the afternoon," I said. "But not me."

"What happened?"

"I got fired."

She gasped. "Oh, my God, what did you do?"

It's funny how people automatically assume that when a person gets fired, they probably deserved it.

I said, "I flipped out, Hill. I took off all my clothes and streaked the president's office. Had my wang hanging out and everything."

"Get out!"

"I'm kidding," I said. "It wasn't my fault. We all got laid off. Including my bosses. It was a merger. A mass suicide. There was nothing anybody could do about it."

"That's *so* late nineties," she said. "Are you all right?"

"Yeah, I'm fine. Nothing a shot of whiskey and a sad Jewel song can't cure."

"Did you tell Mr. Perfect yet?"

"Not yet. I'll call him in a little while. Maybe tomorrow. I think he's off for the holidays then. But you know what he's going to say."

There was a long pause on the line, giving us both a moment to reflect on Mr. Perfect. That's what we called our father. He was a very good man, but he suffered from one particular disease that drove us both crazy. He was right all the time. And I do mean *all* the time. So you could never argue with him. Not on anything. If you did, you would only come away frustrated. He never wanted me to go into banking, saying that it was a low-paying job in an unsteady field. Instead, he'd urged me to follow him into life insurance. As much as he might have been right on this one, I just couldn't picture myself talking about death all day. It upsets me.

In my sister's case, it had been her choice of cars. She had insisted on buying an old VW van despite his warnings. He had suggested a sensible Toyota or some other reliable Japanese vehicle rated high by *Consumer Reports*. Something that wouldn't break down on you when you needed it the most. But my sister—being big on the cool quotient at the time—said driving a used Honda was almost as unhip as wearing designer-label clothes.

Hillary was currently into this whole retro hippie thing: bellbottom jeans, plum-red sweaters, and peace sign chokers. Her brown hair was long and straight, and she insisted on little or no makeup. But she didn't need any. She was blessed with simple beauty and a big heart. And that's what I loved most about my sister—her big heart. She was an aspiring author and a senior majoring in creative writing at Bennington College. Mr. Perfect thought her major was broadcast journalism. That's what he thought he was paying for anyway. A future TV broadcaster with a fat contract. If Hill would have told him the truth, he probably would've flipped out. I guarantee he would've stopped the tuition money.

Mr. Perfect liked art, but it was for other people's children to major in. Not his. He had lectured her over and over on how hard it is to make a living in the arts. The odds of making it were just too great, he'd said. "Open up a gift basket business, sweetheart, and you won't get hurt."

I admired my sister for going after her dreams, and I loved her very much. She was funny and talented and she wrote me nice poems that made me feel proud that I had a sister. She also had a knack for making me feel better when I needed it the most.

A moment later she said, "Don't be so blue, Stu. You'll find another job. People like you."

"Liking people and paying people are two different things, Hillary." I changed the subject quickly. "So what's wrong with the van?"

"I feel so bad about asking you, now that you've lost your job."

"That's what a big bro is for," I said. And I meant it. I would do anything for my sister. *Anything.* But first I had to ask it.

"What about that spiritual boyfriend of yours? The religion major ... Harry. I mean doesn't that guy ever have any dough?"

"He does," she said, "but he's saving it for us."

"What's more important than fixing the van?"

"New Year's Day 2001," she said. "The official dawn of the new millennium. Harry thinks it's the end of the world, so he wants to go out in style. We're booking our reservations early. It's either huddling in mass at St. Peter's Basilica in Rome, hiking up to Peru's Machu Picchu, or ascending the Mount of Olives. We haven't decided yet."

"Why doesn't the little pilgrim just do us all a big favor," I said, "and jump into a volcano. I'm sure Mount Etna would be happy to oblige." Silence struck the line. As much as she loved me, she hated it when I made fun of her significant other. "How much do you need?" I asked.

"Nine hundred dollars," she said, holding her breath. "Supposedly it's a discount."

I didn't quibble with the amount. Any car that had been engineered in 1968 would be a minimum of a grand at every stop.

"Can you wait two days?" I asked, knowing that sending a check FedEx would cost me ten dollars and Priority Mail two. I was already counting pennies. Something you learn how to do real quick when you're out of a job. I mean it doesn't take you long to start stealing toilet paper from gas stations or lifting those extra napkins from McDonald's. You wait and see. When the cash flow stops, you do what you gotta do.

"I love you so much, big brother," she said. "And if you need to talk … call me."

"I love you too," I said. "Now go get your wheels fixed, because I want to see that big beautiful van in the driveway by Christmas." I could hear her smiling on the other end of the line.

"Thanks, big bro," she said. "Have a happy Thanksgiving, and I'll see you in a few weeks … bye."

I hung up the phone and made myself another drink. I decided I wasn't going to call Mr. Perfect until tomorrow. It was only three in the afternoon on Monday, and if he received a non-emergency call during working hours, he'd freak. He was one of those schedule nuts. Besides, he'd already wished me a happy birthday this morning, so there would be no need for him to call back today. And even if he did, I wouldn't answer.

I'm a big call-screener.

For the next three hours I just sat there in the living room of my one-bedroom apartment, sipping Tanqueray and tonic, and listening to classic rock. Every so often I'd take inventory of my surroundings: cream leatherette couches, cheap Swedish furniture, and some old Japanese paintings that I had acquired from some rich guy's garage sale in Marina del Rey. It wasn't much of a pad, but it was mine. And for the first time I realized that it was a luxury I was going to have to hang on to. Maybe even fight for.

I was terrified of the future, frozen, putting off writing that check to my sister. I knew now that once I'd subtracted the nine "large ones" from my current balance, I'd be left with less than twenty-three hundred dollars in my bank account. Barely a month's worth of bills.

I would be broke in thirty days.

I CALLED MR. Perfect the next morning. He answered like he always did. Soft on the "hell." Heavy on the "O."

"Hell-OOOO."

"Hey, Dad," I said. "I have some news."

I don't know why I led off with that "have some news" line. I really don't. It made me sound like a terrorist—some covert nut just in from a successful throat slashing.

"Well good morning, son," he said. "What's up?"

There's never an easy way for a son to tell his father that he is a failure, so the best route is always the direct one.

"Got laid off, Dad. The bank got bought out, and Frontier Savings and Loan is history … I'm out of a job."

There was a long, scary, deep silence on the other end of the line. Then I heard the phone drop. Three seconds later I heard him screaming at the top of his lungs. "Jeeeeeezuuuussss! … Aaaitch! … KeeeeRIST! What kind of news is that?"

I knew he'd have this type of reaction, so I just weathered the storm until he collected himself. (Which as it turned out was only a couple of "Holy molys!" later.) When he did finally pick up the receiver, his breathing labored, he delivered the words I had been expecting, although dreading.

"I think this qualifies as one of the biggest I-told-you-sos of the twentieth century ... don't you agree?"

Mr. Perfect was big on I-told-you-sos, and although you could see them coming from a mile away, the words never failed to pierce your heart.

"Nobody can predict the future, Dad," I said. "It's just something that happened."

"I can," he said, "and did. Everybody dies ... didn't I tell you this would happen?"

"I don't want to argue with you, Dad. I just thought you should know." I paused. "In case you wanted to help."

"Are you asking me for money?" he said. "Is that it?"

"No," I said. "I just thought you might have some ideas about my job search ... anything but insurance."

I heard him take a deep sigh of relief. You see, Mr. Perfect had an understanding with money. He didn't fuck with it, and it didn't fuck with him. All others be damned in their little agreement. So, needless to say, telling him about my current financial crisis would only upset that arrangement. (As well as possibly induce an earth-shattering coronary.)

"Good," my father said, "then you're okay money-wise for a while, right? I mean you did put away that six-month reserve like I told you ... *right?*"

"Of course, Dad," I said, lying through my teeth. "I'm sittin' fat. The perfect picture of financial health."

Medic!

After the initial shock of the news had worn off and the money end had been discussed, Mr. Perfect resumed normal functions. It was always amazing to me how nice and clever and concerned he could be once the money issue had been resolved. He enjoyed plotting and planning, and if he ever wrote a book, I would insist on the title *The*

Machinations of Mr. Perfect. No doubt its collection of meticulous musings would be destined for the bestseller lists.

"Despite what people tell you," he said, "the holidays are an excellent time to search for work. Most companies have already set their budgets and would just as soon fill their empty slots by the new year. And I have just the man for you to call. His name is Jolly Marks."

"Sounds like a circus clown to me," I said.

Mr. Perfect raised his voice. "That is exactly the kind of bad attitude that will leave you stranded out in the streets, son. So you'd better lose it, or you will not survive out there."

"Okay, okay, I know," I said, quickly veering him away from the lecture path.

"Mr. Marks just happens to run one of the finest employment search firms in Los Angeles," he said. "He owes me a favor, and I'm sure he'll meet with you tomorrow."

"Is he a client?" I asked. "Or did you meet him at one of your *parties?*"

"I met him at the Easter bash I threw last year," he said. "He impressed me as someone who knew a lot about the changing job market."

"Not the guy who drew a triangle with a Magic Marker on your refrigerator door?"

"That's him. The hierarchy-of-a-job-search guy. And you will meet with him tomorrow ... that's an order."

Mr. Perfect threw a lot of parties. Mostly for networking purposes. He enjoyed the tax write-off as well as the hunt for new business. Since he sold whole life select preferred insurance policies, all of the guests, or "prospective applicants," depending on how you looked at it, had been thoroughly screened for preexisting health conditions. (Without their knowledge or consent of course.)

Thanks to a group of progressive doctors in La Mirada, my father was able to obtain sensitive health information on just about anybody with a simple click of the mouse. "Information wants to be free, Hudson." Those were his exact words.

Each week he would e-mail a list of one hundred prospects to the doctors, and within minutes, he would receive chemical profiles, cholesterol levels, and blood pressure readings. This information was then used to identify the smokers, diabetics, crackheads, boozehounds, and all those with a history of cancer in their families. All big no-no's to an insurance man's bottom line.

"Besides," the old man had said, "no use wasting a good salmon roll on somebody who can't taste it."

Once the weak had been identified, their names were promptly deleted from the files. All others made the guest list. It was as simple as that. Including the doctors—who were always feted in grand style. (There were rumors of backroom hookers, but don't quote me on that.)

"After all," my father had said, "if there's one thing I've learned in sales, son, it's not how many leads you have, but how many *qualified* leads you have."

Needless to say, Mr. Perfect's parties were a trip. I'll take you to one later, but first I want to get back to Jolly Marks. The guy who evidently acted like a full-on nimrod in my father's kitchen.

As I recall, on that one particular Easter Sunday, I arrived late at my father's house to find a dissected triangle drawn on his olive-colored refrigerator door. Looking closer, I noticed that it was divided into four sections. At the large base of the pyramid were the written words, "SEARCH FIRM." This naturally comprised the biggest piece of the "pie." Naturally. The second tier had the word, "FRIENDS," the third, "CLASSIFIEDS," and the tip of the triangle was labeled "FAMILY." Evidently, Mr. Marks had performed this little demonstration in response to Mr. Perfect's query, "So what do you do, Jolly?" (By the way, get used to fielding this question when you're unemployed. It always seems to crop up when you're out of a job. Cocktail parties. Holidays. High school reunions. All can be quite hell when you've got squat on the horizon. Astronaut school was one of my early favorites.) Mr. Marks then went on to explain to my father his hierarchy-of-a-job-search theory, with the bottom line basically being: *you really do need my services, so pay me when you got the dough.* I have to admit I wasn't real keen on meeting anybody who drew on refrigerator doors, but I had few options left at the time.

"All right," I said. "What's his number? I'll call the guy."

My father gave me the digits and ordered, "Ring him immediately. And report back to me *ASAP*. And ... son?"

"Yeah, Dad?"

"It's time to get tough. Pull up your socks and dig in."

"Whatever."

-6-

MR. MARKS AGREED to meet me on Wednesday afternoon—one day before Turkey Day. When I arrived at his tiny Westside office at two sharp, our agreed-upon time, I was immediately assaulted by a robotic, middle-aged woman with upswept blonde hair and a fashionable dress the color of blue ice. I kept my distance at first, although she seemed pleasant enough. Not like she was foaming at the mouth or anything.

"It's such a pleasure to meet you, Mr. Foster," she said. "I'm Mrs. Showorthy. Please have a seat and fill this out." She handed me a clipboard with a questionnaire attached. Then we somehow managed to shake hands.

"Once you have completed it," she said, "bring it over to the reception window. I'll pass it along to Mr. Marks for evaluation." A mechanical smile lit up her programmed face.

"Thank you," I said. I took a seat on a floral armchair in the reception area and studied the questionnaire. It was filled with a lot of personal questions. Questions asking me about my age, dislikes and likes, job history, personality quirks, lifestyle, and future plans. I mean, it was like I was trying to get a damn date with the Queen of England or something.

To be honest with you, I felt a little uncomfortable. I answered everything though—that is, until the very last page. The financial page. The page wanting to know how much money I had in the bank. How much my stock portfolio was worth, and how much real estate I owned. But it was the last question that made my skin crawl. It read: "*Please check the appropriate box that best describes your liquid assets available now. $0-3,000. $3,000-5,000. $5,000-15,000. $15,000+.*"

I left it blank. In fact, I left the whole friggin' section blank. I wasn't about to disclose my financials to anyone on the first visit. Especially since I was in the $0-3,000 category and dwindling fast. I mean I still had my pride, right? I was a professional, damn it.

I signed the application and walked up to the dividing window, then handed it back to the receptionist. "Thank you," she said. "Please have a seat. Mr. Marks will be with you in a moment."

I nodded politely and sat back down, staring blankly out the window at the falling rain. It gave me a moment to look back over the last forty-eight hours. It had been hellish, the range of emotions wide, although quite productive. I put together my resume using an old book that I'd had since high school, and I'd finally written that check out and sent it off to my sister. Then I called a couple of "old" friends and broke the news to them about my current employment status, thus effectively putting out the feelers for a new job.

Everyone was sympathetic but not overly concerned. That happens to you when you get close to thirty, I guess. You've got your own problems to deal with, so you learn how to show people you care without getting too emotionally involved. It's called conserving energy—or protecting your butt. Because I have come to realize that the older you get, the higher the stakes get. That's just the way it is. When you're young, job recommendations come free and easy. Handed out like cake at a birthday party. That's because most people don't have anything to lose at that age. But once you hit the big three-o, guys have to start factoring in families and shit. How will recommending this person for a job affect my reputation? My career? My social standing? I'm telling you all this now, because when you get out there, you'll know why most of these so-called "old beer buddies" aren't that excited to open new doors for you. Only the truly loyal will do that. So don't blame those poor saps who don't run to your rescue when you need it the most. They're just scared. Scared of losing what they've got. And it's a shame, too, because the fear of loss always stands in the way of many a would-be Good Samaritan. Besides, as my father once said, the statute of limitations on old friendships usually runs out after seven years.

"Mr. Foster! It is such a pleasure to meet you!"

I'll never forget the moment Jolly Marks burst in and broke my daydream. His voice was so loud and full of vaudevillian schmaltz it made my insides shake.

"You must be Mr. Marks," I said, standing up and shaking his hand.

"Please," said the seventy-year-old man, two-stepping and waving his arms like he was auditioning for a dance number. "Call me Jolly."

Ba-dum-bum.

"Okay," I said. "Jolly it is."

This guy was a real gem, I thought. A Mel Brooks look-alike and the shtick to match. He was dressed real dapper in a dark Brooks Brothers suit, and his mostly bald head was split in two by a thin racing stripe of gray hair. But it was that damned energetic smile on his face and the naughty twinkle in his eye that made him look younger than his years. I gotta admit, he kinda scared me.

He stood in the doorway, motioning with his hand like a

matador teasing a bull. "Please follow me, Hudson. It's time to find you a new job."

Ba-dum-bum.

We walked down the red-carpeted hallway, and he looked over his shoulder and said, "By the way, kid, that's a hell of a nice shine you got on those shoes. Your pop teach you that?"

"Yeah, he did," I said, suddenly feeling gushy without knowing why.

"Hell of a nice guy, your old man," he said. "Throws a great party. And great food. The salmon rolls are insane."

"That's because they're free," I said.

Mr. Marks laughed and wagged a playful finger in my direction. "Looks like you've inherited his dry wit as well. That's an asset. Come on, Hudson. Let's hook you up."

He ushered me into his plush office, and we sat down. His office was located on the seventh floor, and his view looked out onto a cluster of high-rise buildings. The rain was still falling, slanting across the sleek glass facades.

Jolly positioned himself behind an executive-type desk and said, "Stand up."

"Excuse me?"

"C'mon," he said, clapping his hands twice, quickly. "Stand up. Let me look at you."

I wasn't real keen on taking orders from strangers. Especially from a guy with his background. But I needed a job. So if he got off on doing the whole guinea pig example routine with me as his subject, then I figured the least I could do was play along. (Up to a point, of course.)

I got up slowly and stood there rigid, wearing this stupid dog grin on my face. I followed him with my eyes as he walked over to me and inspected my clothes, circling my body like some exasperated fashion designer. Then he made a snapping sound with his cheek and gums and started shaking his head in disgust.

"What?" I asked. *"What?"*

"The gray suit is adequate at best," he said. "And I'm afraid the off-the-rack chic of the early nineties is over."

"But you like the shoes, right? I mean you said the shoes were good."

"I said the shine was good, son. I didn't say I *liked* the shoes. But they'll do for now. Personally, I don't like wingtips. They scream low-level management. But that's just me. I'm more of a cap-toe kind of guy."

He fingered my red paisley tie. "Nice silk. A little thin. But it'll do." Another look. Another sigh. "The button-down has to go, son. Button-down shirts are for college kids and accountants only. And you, my friend, are neither." He forced a thin smile. "I think it's time to stop shopping at Macy's and step up to Bloomingdale's, don't you think? I mean, if I can be brutally honest with you, Hudson, a seventy-thousand-dollar-a-year job offer does not come to one dressed like this. I suggest flipping through the latest *GQ* or *Esquire* to give you some fashion ideas. It'll make all the difference in the world."

I felt my temper starting to boil. And I swear to God, I was *this close* to making him the cover shot of next month's *Knuckle Sandwich* magazine. But I held it in, opting for the more civilized approach. After all, I told myself, one mustn't be too sensitive when seeking employment.

"I'm afraid Bloomingdale's is a little out of my price range right now," I said.

He smiled, albeit a touch grimly. "Yes, well," he said, walking back behind his desk and sitting down, "do keep it in mind for the future."

I sensed something had happened there, but I wasn't sure what. Was he probing me? I sat down as he put on a pair of glasses and studied my resume. It had been faxed to him early that morning at his request. He said he liked to have a resume at least three hours in advance. That way he could get a feel for the applicant and start charting a preliminary career path.

Jolly cleared his throat, then looked up at me through his old-man reading glasses. "When did you do this resume?"

"Yesterday," I said. "Why?"

"It looks old, tired." He shook his corn-rowed forehead, crumpled up the paper, and baseballed it into a nearby trash can. "This *stinks.*"

"I was in kind of a hurry," I said. "Under pressure. You know how it is."

"Yes, I do," he said flatly.

Jolly stood up, expressionless, and walked over to the bookshelf. He leaned against it and wiped down his reading glasses with a tissue. "Do you know what we do here at Niche Finders International, Mr. Foster?"

"Yeah," I said. "You're a headhunter."

Jolly frowned and pointed a bony finger at me. "No," he said, "we are *not a* headhunter. We are a *service.* So, please, do not use the word *head* around me again." (I wouldn't think of it.) "Because it has nothing to do with who we are here." I watched his older body quiver at the thought of it.

"Then what does your service do?" I asked.

"Simply put," he said, "we search the world for you. The hierarchy of a job search begins and ends right here with our firm. We are the base of the pyramid, son. Your foundation." He threw up his hands and smiled. "And what do we search for, you ask? A job? Money? Power? Benefits? A shorter commute? No, my friend," he said, walking about the room now and rubbing his hands together greedily. "We search for what every man seeks."

"And what is that?" I asked.

He stopped at the window for a moment and watched the falling rain. Then he came at me with a soft voice full of wisdom. "Your ultimate niche, Mr. Foster. Your God-given niche." He turned and faced me, his eyes glowing bright. *"Your destiny."*

I didn't know it at the time, but this guy was really leading me down there. Setting me up for the kill. He was good. Real good.

"How do you know when you find it?" I asked, sounding like a gee-whiz moron. "The niche, I mean."

"We just know, Mr. Foster. Because we know that once we find a person's true calling in this world, then we know that health, wealth, and happiness will follow. It's a time-tested formula. And one that will work for you. That's what we do here at Niche Finders International, Mr. Foster. We give you the world." He smiled like an evil circus clown. "Simply put, we make dreams come true."

"Sounds like Niche Finders is the place for me."

I couldn't have sounded more geeky.

"Sounds like it," said Jolly. He walked back over to his desk and rifled through a drawer. Then he pulled out the classifieds section of the *Los Angeles Times* and sat back down. "Now that you know what we do here … it's time to take the first step. Which leads me back to your resume." He slid the newspaper across the desk and said, "Flip to the automobile section of the classifieds. Go to BMW cars. Tell me what you see?"

I picked up the paper and stared at it a moment. I said, "It looks like a bunch of old car ads to me. Prices. Lease payments. Basic stuff."

"Basic stuff—*exactly*," said Jolly with a sly smile. "Just like your resume, Hudson." He pulled out a colored brochure from his desk drawer and slid it across the desktop. "Take a look at that." I studied the slick presentation. It had glossy pictures of BMWs with fancy writing and a bunch of arty shots of the leather interior.

"See the difference?" he asked. "They're the same cars as in the newspaper. Same prices. Same everything. Just packaged differently."

"You're talking about marketing," I said.

"Not just marketing, Hudson. But *glitz. Hype. Glamour. Pop.* Now that's what sells. It's called appeal, son. And you, my friend, have none of it." He shook his head. "Unfortunately, *you are* the classifieds."

I was starting to get a little PO'd by now. I'd figured out that Uncle Jolly's whole "glamorous" routine was canned, a thin circus act performed daily to entertain and woo potential clients.

"I get your point," I said, a little edge creeping up in my voice now. "But my bank account is shrinking as we speak. So can we get to the meat of the matter, Jolly? Frankly, I need a paycheck, not a show."

I watched him cringe, then lean back in his chair and steeple his hands. "Before I get to that," he said, "I think we should talk about my up-front fee."

"Fee?" I said. "I wasn't aware of any fees, Jolly."

"The fine print is written on all our literature," he said.

"I didn't see any literature. I was referred by my father."

He held up a company brochure and pointed at the very fine print at the bottom of the page. "You see?"

I took the brochure from his outstretched hand and held it up to my face, squinting. The print was so fine it looked like an ink spot: "fee req'd."

"Jesus Christ, Jolly!" I said. "What the hell is that? Minus-one-point font? How do you expect anybody to read that?"

The old buzzard flashed me a tight business smile. "Do you

think I work for free?" He leaned forward, his elbows on the desk. "Look, Mr. Foster, as you know, my firm goes to great lengths to find someone their ultimate niche. And finding the ultimate niche takes time and money. Sometimes up to a year."

He sat up in his chair, crossed his arms, and gave it to me straight. "My up-front fee is $5,000. That's excluding postage, phone, and the very expensive lunches at the Ivy that I must endure to sell you. And let's face it: you're not getting any younger. By corporate standards today, you're over the hill by age forty. But, if you were in a hot field, such as technology or health care, then maybe I would consider taking you on at a lower price." He shook his head gloomily. "But I'm afraid your field of banking is not a very hot market right now. Banking, as we know it, is dead. Just like George Bailey and the old Building and Loan. So, in lieu of a very long speech about the future of our financial institutions, I think it's only fair to warn you about this up front."

I was just about to let the old bastard have it with a stinging barb when his secretary walked in and said, "Here's Mr. Foster's completed personality profile, Mr. Marks."

Jolly took the clipboard from her hand and said, "Thank you, Mrs. Showorthy. That'll be all." The secretary left the room, and Jolly said, "Give me just a moment to review your file, Hudson. Maybe there is something in here that can help change my mind."

I nodded and watched the old man turn right to the financial page. Jolly didn't look so jolly. He took a deep breath, then took off his reading glasses and rubbed his wrinkly eyes. "I'm going to be brutally honest with you, Hudson. Get to the meat of the matter as you say. I don't think I can help you."

"What do you mean?" I asked. "Over the phone, you said you had lots of employers seeking good applicants. There's nobody better than me."

"The competition is fierce, son. I have grown men with families seeking these positions. And young chargers who will work for peanuts. And, frankly, bad hires are terribly expensive. I'm afraid I can't take that chance."

I jumped up from my chair and yelled, "I bet if I had twenty grand in my bank account, you'd take that chance!"

"Now, Hudson, there is no need to get heated. This is just the type of rejection that most interviews bring. Use this experience wisely and learn from it."

I was so mad I wanted to strangle him. Not because he couldn't find me a job, but because he hadn't disclosed his fee to me up front before the interview. You see, that's what these headhunters do. They manipulate you. They know that if they told you how and what they charged for their services, you wouldn't come down for an interview. So they tell you everything you want to hear over the phone to get you into their office. Then they have you fill out this long questionnaire about yourself, but the only thing they really want to know is how much dough you've got. Because the whole scam is based on your ability to pay them. That's why Jolly Marks went right to my financial page. He didn't give a shit about me or my "leadership qualities." He just wanted to scan my bank accounts. The bastard. I know now that my leaving the financial section blank told him all that he needed to know. That I was broke. So his response became automatic pilot after that. *I don't think I can help you.* I wondered how many qualified applicants had sat there before me and had been told those very same words because their bank accounts were too thin. Well, I'll tell you one thing: I wasn't going to let the old bastard off the hook that easy. So I decided to raise his blood pressure a notch.

The old swindler deserved it.

"You know what you are?" I said with fire in my eyes.

"Oh, no, please," begged Jolly, realizing he had a live one on his hands. "Don't say it. Please don't say it."

"You're a goddamn flesh peddler!" I said. "A no-good *headhunter!*"

"No," he said, waving his hands in resignation. "Please ... NO!"

I leaned in face-to-face and repeated it several times. "Headhunter! Headhunter! HEADHUNTER!" Then I gritted my teeth and pounded the desk, and his cheesy pen and pencil set crashed to the floor.

His face went white, and beads of sweat rolled off his aged forehead. He panicked and smashed the intercom button. "Security, please!"

Jesus, I thought, that was twice in one week. I was starting to feel like a real outlaw now. I decided I'd better ease off on the old coot before he stroked out on me, so I walked for the door.

"Don't sweat it, Uncle Jolly," I said. "I'm leaving. But just remember one thing. Be straight up with people from now on, or it will come back to haunt you. It's called karma."

Just as I was about to leave the room, I thought of something else and turned in the doorway.

"By the way, pal. You can kiss those salmon rolls goodbye. You're off the A-list."

-7-

I DIDN'T KNOW it at the time, but that day was only the beginning. The downsizing of Hudson Foster had begun. After that charming interview with Mr. Marks, I remember hopping into my car and driving west on Wilshire Boulevard. The rain was still falling, and the congested street was slick and noisy with traffic.

I was hungry and my wallet was empty, so I decided to stop at the local bank and withdraw a five-spot.

The teller said, "Gettin' a little gas money, huh?"

"Yup," I said, playing along. "Just trying to get from here to there. Nothing more." But what I was really thinking about at the time was how I was going to stretch this fiver till Thanksgiving.

That's the secret, you know, making your money go a long way. That's why I stopped at the bank instead of the ATM. Most ATMs only give you twenties. And if you withdraw twenties, then you're going to spend twenties.

I didn't want to do it, but I knew I had no choice. I was going to have to stick to a poor man's budget. Arco AM-PM lunch specials. Late-night runs to the Food 4 Less. And worse yet, slinking out of Walgreens like Mata Hari with dark sunglasses, a twelver of Meister Brau tucked conspicuously under my arm.

It was a far cry from champagne nights and caviar dreams.

Later on I went to the corner pay phone and dialed up Mr. Perfect. I decided to get it over with—fill him in as he'd instructed. He answered, as always, on the half ring.

"Hell-OOOO."

"Dad, it's me."

"How'd it go?" Mr. Perfect was in no mood for fluff.

"The guy's a real quack, Dad," I said, adjusting my umbrella. "Why didn't you tell me he charged five grand for his services … up front?"

"He wanted *five thousand dollars*?"

"Yeah."

Mr. Perfect fell silent, but I could still hear him and his money having a heated inner conversation. It didn't last long. They both agreed quickly. "Well, he can forget about the Christmas party," he finally said. "The no-good charlatan."

"Yeah, that's what I told him."

Mr. Perfect sighed. "It looks like we're down to friends and family, son. What about your buddy Gardner? He's a stable guy. Well connected. Maybe he might have some job ideas for you."

"Yeah, I'm going over there in a little while. He said he might know of an opportunity."

"Good," he said. "So what are you doing for Thanksgiving tomorrow? You gonna carve the bird with your old man?"

"Who you havin' over?"

"My staff and their families. Big PR move."

Mr. Perfect viewed every holiday as an opportunity to increase business.

"Pass," I said. "Gardner's having me over." Which wasn't true. I just wanted to be alone for the holiday. Lose myself in booze, football games, and self-pity. I knew that, come December 1, the real ax of reality would come crashing down. Rent was due. The car payment and credit card bills were due. It would be a very black time.

"All right," said Mr. Perfect. "But just remember the Christmas party is on the twenty-fourth this year. I've got a lot of clients and prospects coming. It'll be an excellent time for you to network. In the meantime, mine your friends for employment leads, and if something doesn't pan out soon, then take a part-time job to tide you over. Mr. Cash Flow is a very fickle character. Once he stops flowing, he finds it very difficult to get started again."

"All right," I said, looking off into the soggy street scene. "And, Dad?"

"Yes."

"You know what I was thinking about? And just hear me out on this one, because it might just make sense."

"Go on."

"Well, I was thinking about filing for unemployment. I think I would qualify for the max. It's something like nine hundred bucks a month."

There was an eerie silence on the other end of the line, the calm before the storm. Then an eruption so powerful it would've rivaled Mount Vesuvius.

"Unacceptable!" he yelled. "Unemployment is for actors and others of that ilk. Not a Foster. A Foster never takes the easy way out. Remember that, son."

"Then I guess bankruptcy is out of the question," I said.

"Don't ever use that word around me again," he said. "People who file for bankruptcy are the same people who are ruining this country."

"But, Dad," I said. "It's in vogue."

I really shouldn't have thrown that last line in. I knew how much it upset Mr. Perfect. But that's how I felt at the time. I had watched others who had led a life of conspicuous consumption, lost their jobs, ran up their credit cards, and, just like that, had wiped away all their debts without one ounce of concern. Then, just like that, they were back in the consumer saddle again, spending money they didn't have, enjoying the high life and knowing full well someone else would foot the bill. It was tough watching people having fun without accountability. I mean, I'm only human. I thought about it myself. It certainly would have been the easy and fun way out. But the easy way out definitely wasn't cool. I guess it all goes back to that old saying: everyone else is doing it. Well, anytime you hear someone validate their own actions by using the words "everyone else is doing it," then don't. Because you're just another lemming jumping off the cliff. And who wants that?

Mr. Perfect said, "You can joke all you want, son. But one day, life is going to hit you over the head. And when it does, I won't be there to bail you out."

"Did I ask for money?"

"You didn't have to," said Mr. Perfect. "Your little BK remark said it all."

"I'm not gonna argue with you, Dad. I already told you, I'm gonna pay you back every cent you ever gave me. *With interest.*"

"You're missing the point, Hudson—"

"Look, Dad, can we talk about this later? I'm standing out on a street corner in the rain. I'll call you later, okay?"

He sighed. "Okay."

He didn't want to argue any more than I did. It made us both tired. That's because we had that argument a lot. Me wanting to pay him back for college and him wanting me to learn more about the value of a dollar. I guess, looking back on it, I was just jealous of his success. Even if he was my own dad. But that's how you get sometimes when you're out of a job. Real defensive. You start barking at people you don't even know, driving like a maniac, and flipping the bird at life in general. So it's best to keep a cool head if you can. I know that sounds like the pot calling the kettle black, and I know that you'd probably rather be getting stoned in front of the TV set or shopping with your friends at some outlet mall rather than reading about some poor old sap who lost his job. But it will happen to you sooner or later in your life. And when it does, you're gonna see what I'm talking about. So just remember the old Boy Scout motto and "be prepared." Because the world has a way of fucking with you when you least expect it.

Something I wasn't aware of yet.

-8-

I ARRIVED AT Gardner's pad a little after six that night. The rain had stopped, and the sky was clear black and full of stars. Gardner lived on Second Street in Santa Monica. A town I do not like very much. It's got all these parking restrictions and meters, and they give tickets twenty-four hours a day. No wonder the locals are always pissed. I call it the high cost of sunshine.

I keyed in Gardner's intercom number, and he buzzed me in. And when I got to the top of the stairs, he greeted me at the front door with two beers in hand.

"The H-man cometh," he said. He handed me a Coors Light and threw me a warm smile.

"What's up, G?" I asked, shaking his hand with several gyrations. I was always happy to see him. Bill Gardner was my best friend. We had met in college, and he had been like a big brother to me. He was two years older than I was, and I really looked up to him. So did a lot of people. He was a "salt of the earth" kind of guy, a perfect cover boy for *Handyman* magazine. Short and thick with a bushy head of brown hair, he had this real comforting voice that always made you feel better when you heard it. Beach casual was his style, and like most native Californians he wore shorts eleven months out of the year. Tonight was no different. He was barefoot and had on a pair of long, black surfer trunks and a big gray sweatshirt that had the bold words "IMPEACH 'EM ALL!" silkscreened in black across his chest. If you were around during the late nineteen nineties, then you might have said he looked a lot like that shaggy-haired comic-strip character Zonker in *Doonesbury.*

But enough about the guy's physical appearance, already. That's not why I'm having you meet Gardner. It's his philosophy of life that counts. And one could learn a lot from a guy like him. I know I did. You see, Gardner came from money. Not billions of dollars, mind you, but enough to live off of a trust fund or work for daddy's real estate company for the rest of his life. But Gardner chose not to go that route. It just wasn't him, he had said, explaining that anything but his own way would be a gross displacement of the soul. So he followed his heart, and for the first five years it had been hell for him. His family had all but disowned him, calling him a loser and a disgrace, and all his wealthy "friends" could say was, "*What a shame.*"

His parents told him that his inheritance would be null and void if he pursued a life of manual labor. But Gardner turned his back on the pressures of conformity and blazed his own path into the world of furniture making. He had always been good with his hands.

Now, ten years later, he was recognized as one of the most successful furniture makers in L.A. The *Los Angeles Times* did a piece on him in the business section not too long ago, touting him as one of the leaders of the new artisan movement. A regular "maestro of wood," they said.

But, as you might have already guessed, there was a dark side to Gardner's success. Everybody wanted a piece of him now, including his parents. They came crawling back with open arms and phony smiles. Because success was (and still is) all that mattered in their small world. *"We knew you could do it, son ... Great job, Gardner. Need an investor?"*

Snobbish bastards.

But Gardner didn't let the hypocrisy bother him. Didn't mind that others were willing to step up and take credit for his success. He was a bigger man than that. And a bigger man than me. Heck, I would have told all those bourgeois bastards where to take it. Shove it right up their ... well, you get the point. But the difference between Gardner and me was that he knew who he was. And once you know who you are, then nothing else matters. That's what Gardner always told me. He said that if you want to do something in life, then do it. No matter how great the odds, no matter that everyone else is against you. Just do it and don't tell anybody. Because there will always be somebody out there just waiting to crush your dream. (A teacher. A parent. A rival.) If you're lucky, you'll have support, but if not, expect a rough road ahead. Dreams can only be attained through hard work and guts. But one of the biggest things that he told me was that failure was my friend. Because after enough of them, you will eventually find success.

"The key is to keep trying," he'd said.

So anytime you find yourself against all odds, gain inspiration from Gardner's story. You're not alone.

Anyhow, Gardner showed me inside his two-bedroom apartment on that day. It was decorated with all his colorful mod furniture and pictures of the Alps in gold frames. I took a seat on a red velvet couch as Gardner headed for the kitchen. He said, "So let's hear it. What happened at the headhunter's office?"

"Service," I said. "And not much. I couldn't afford his fee. I think those flesh peddlers are all in on the conspiracy."

Gardner laughed. "The guy gave you the old service crap, huh?

Probably made you feel like you weren't worthy of his representation. Then gave you some big song and dance before he got to the bottom line—your ability to pay." He rustled pots and pans near the sink. "That's classic."

"You heard it before?"

"Heard it all before."

"Then why didn't you tell me?"

"There are certain things in life that one must find out on his own," said Gardner.

"Like what?"

"Like how to recognize a racket when you see one."

Gardner stepped out of the kitchen and into the living room, drying off a dish. He's one of those guys who's always doing something while he talks to you. Peeling onions (he likes to cook), hanging Christmas lights, or carting laundry to and fro. He never loses focus on the conversation though, his big almond eyes rotating sincerely between you and his project.

"You see, Hudson, there are only two kinds of headhunters in this world—those that charge an up-front fee … and those that don't. The ones that charge a fee have to convince you that they're worth what they're charging. Once they do that, then they will go to work for you. Even if they don't have an employer that matches your criteria."

"Then what you're sayin' is … is that most of the time their connections might be just as good as mine?"

"Bingo," said Gardner, walking back into the kitchen and retrieving a new dish. "All they do is contact employers on your behalf, wooing you with big dreams of the hidden job market. They only have so many contacts. After that, it's the standard cold call. There's no such thing as a hidden job market. It doesn't exist to the unconnected."

"Come to think of it," I said, "the guy did tell me it could take up to a year to find me work. Of course, that was before he found out about my financials."

Gardner chuckled. "Of course he did. After he gets your fee, then he's got a year to tell you that he's very sorry he couldn't help you out. He'll start going off about how long the average job search takes, and how every man should have at least six to nine months in cash reserves to sustain him through the hard times. If he finds out that his potential client is cash-poor, then he politely bows out. That's why a fee-charging agency only works for top-level executives. Gullible white guys with cash. CEOs, CFOs, CIOs, and other senior administrators. It's strictly a revenue-driven business now. So face it, if you're not rich and white, then they won't find you a job. It's one of the biggest rackets known to mankind."

"So what about the ones that don't charge a fee?"

"The employers pay them, or they get part of your first year's salary when they place you."

I crossed my hands behind my head and leaned back on the couch. "Now that sounds more like it."

Gardner brought his dish over to an overstuffed chair and sat down, his gnarled hands vigorously polishing the plate's shiny surface. There was a confident twinkle in his eye now, a twinkle that suggested he'd seen the business world from both ends of the stick.

"The headhunters that don't charge a fee are a waste of time for those looking for work," he said. "They work for the masses, the grunts, anybody making under fifty thousand a year. And since they don't get paid by you, they'll take the path of least resistance. It's a one-way ticket to a McJob."

I leaned forward, feeling pangs of anger. "What do you mean?

I'm just the kind of guy who keeps them in business."

"Maybe," said Gardner, his finger raised to make a point, the tone of his voice like that of a monk close to nirvana. "But you must remember that, since they don't charge an up-front fee, they are inundated with resumes from eager candidates just like yourself, who are desperately looking for work. This gives them the luxury of time and choice. Something you as a job seeker don't have."

"Well, how do I stand out above the crowd?"

"Salary for one," said Gardner. "The other is having a job."

"Having a job! C'mon!" I said. "I'm going to the goddamn place to get a job!"

"But that's not what they want. Most of the time they are hired by the companies. And the companies tell them what they're looking for and how much they're willing to pay. According to them, the best candidates are already employed. So the service earns its money by poaching. Or luring away top executives from other like firms. So you see, Hudson, they don't want people who don't have jobs. It's just like banks. They only want to lend money to people who don't need it."

"So where does that leave me?"

"Much better off," answered Gardner, cruising back into the kitchen at tugboat speed. "Don't pay someone for work you can do yourself, Hudson. Headhunters are a waste of time and money today, unless you know one personally. They're no different from any other salesman. You're strictly a commission in their eyes."

I shifted uneasily on the couch, absorbing the information I had just been so gratuitously handed. Gardner was right. Jobs didn't magically appear anymore. (That is, unless you were willing to clean a hotel room for minimum wage.) You had to go after them. Get aggressive. Like a terrier hunts a fox.

"Any suggestions on where to start?" I asked.

"You still want to stay in banking?"

"I don't know," I said. "Maybe something different. I know people say search in your same field, but I'm still not sure."

Gardner entered the room and handed me a glass of water. He knew one beer was my limit if I was driving. Even then, I waited an hour for it to burn off.

"I've got a lead for you."

My eyes widened. "You do?"

"Actually it comes from Maxine."

Maxine, or Max, as we called her, was Gardner's wife. She was a great lady, real good people. She worked for the Walt Disney Company in the animation department, but she didn't have that snooty attitude that most entertainment executives have in this town. Something I found real refreshing.

Gardner continued. "Supposedly, a friend of a friend of one of her ex-coworkers is starting a new financial software company. First Financial Technologies. The guy's saying he's going to revolutionize the way people get home loans. He's looking for sales reps. We don't know any more than that, but Max told him you might be interested. Are you?"

"Are you kidding me? Yes! That would be great! Do you have his number?"

"No."

"No?"

"No. But I have his address." Gardner smiled. "You have an interview on Friday afternoon at two. It's all set up. That is, unless you've got better things to do."

I'm gonna tell you something right now. Good friends like Gardner and his old lady don't come around all that often. So you'd better appreciate them while you can. Because when you're a teenager or in your twenties, it's so easy to make friends. For some, it's their high school buddies; for others, it's their college chums who stick with them for life. Oh, you may meet a few soul mates along the way, but you never really connect the way you do when you're young. Because the bond of the playground is always stronger than any office steel. You'll find that out later.

"That's fantastic," I said. "I really appreciate the opportunity."

"No problem," Gardner said. "Call us after the interview and let us know how it went. And about Thanksgiving," he added, "you want to join us?"

Gardner wanted to dress up in one of those big pilgrim hats and shoot his own turkey at some farm up near Bakersfield. We had a lot of things in common, but that wasn't one of them.

"No," I said. "I think I'm going to take it easy. Get some rest and prepare for the interview."

"Have it your way."

I shook his strong hand and walked for the door.

"Thanks again for the lead, Gardner. And be sure and thank your wife for me, will ya?"

"Anytime, bro."

-9-

THANKSGIVING CAME AND went, and by Friday I was ready to start a new life. The offices of First Financial Technologies were located in Westchester, near the airport. I got there about a quarter to two the next afternoon. I didn't want to be late. It's always better to be early than late. That way you can fix up your hair, scope out the environment, or search out a free parking space. Because one of the first rules of job hunting on a tight budget is to never park in the building—unless you know it's free. People don't validate anymore. It's just another sign of the times. And believe me, the last thing you need after a bad interview with a bald man is a bill for fifteen bucks from some grubby parking company.

Fortunately, I didn't have to worry about parking on that day. The dilapidated two-story brick building was positioned next to a dusty construction site, and like an old-fashioned drive-up motel, spaces were readily available in front. I pulled the car in and noticed the first floor was occupied by a pet food store. First Financial must be on the second floor, I thought. Or hoped. But I didn't let it bother me too much. I knew that most start-ups were low on capital.

The instant I exited the vehicle, the dry smell of construction dust and cat hair hammered my senses. (A prime example of why most mixed-use properties rarely turned a profit.) The elevator was out of order and the entrance to the stairs was blocked off for painting, so I had no choice but to take the catwalk up to the second floor. It was a warm late fall day, and I could already feel a light sweat blossoming underneath my suit. Climbing up the steel ladder, with briefcase in hand and dark Ray-Ban sunglasses high on my nose, I felt curious eyes upon me.

People were staring.

But why?

I wanted to shout down at them, *"Hey, people! You got a problem? You never seen a guy in a suit before?"* But I didn't. I just kept climbing up that ladder with purpose, like some bad seventies villain in a *Mod Squad* episode—nervous and twitchy, head snapping in all directions. I could almost hear the cheesy soundtrack accompanying my frantic ascent.

Then I imagined people talking about me.

"What do you think, Herbie. He a federal agent? FBI?"

"No. Too clean. Probably an interviewee. Some guy looking for a job."

"The poor sap."

"Tell me about it."

There was an easy way to pick out the unemployed at the turn of the century. It was called "casual Friday." A dress code I would come to loathe. It used to be that I'd be a normal guy in a suit ready for a hard day's work. But not anymore. I was a greenhorn now. A pledge in a new millennial fraternity … someone who had not yet earned the right to wear a pair of khakis and a T-shirt to work.

I felt like a real Biff, I tell ya, a real Biff.

When I got to the top of the stairs, I took a deep breath and smoothed my hair back in the window. Then I pointed at my reflection and mouthed the mantra, *"Let's rock."*

The second I opened the office door, I smelled dead animals.

"Phew," I said, my eyes watering.

"You'll get used to it," said a lumpy red-haired secretary. "Just pretend you're at the zoo. It works for me."

I took a step forward in the small reception area. After a moment, my eyes cleared. There wasn't much to see. Just the pudgy secretary seated at a cluttered desk and a black beanbag chair.

"I'm Hudson Foster," I said. "I have a two o'clock with Mr. Plano."

A gap-toothed smile emerged. "Shirley Haphazard. Nice to meet you." We shook hands. "I'll let him know you're here," she said. "And please excuse the mess. We're brand-new. Just moved in. And as you can see, we're still waiting on furniture."

I launched a killer grin. "And I thought you were going for that whole minimalism thing."

A cigarette laugh shook from her burrito-like body. My cue to chuckle along. I had learned never to underestimate the power of a secretary. They're the ones who open doors.

I watched Shirley pick up the phone and announce my presence. It gave me a moment to study a possible coworker. She was wearing an ASU sweatshirt that matched her red hair. (Immediate points given for being a Pac-12 woman.) She looked about forty, with a crusty white face, but noticing the pack of Kools on the desk, I figured her for about thirty. Had her pegged for the kind of gal you'd see waiting in a lottery line outside of a Gardena liquor store—a bowling-alley babe with a hankering for road trips and Powerball.

"He'll be with you in a moment," she said, hanging up the phone. "Please have a seat."

"Thanks," I said.

Just as I turned she said, "Candy?"

I saw her hold up a decorative basket. "They're really quite good," she said. "Chocolate-covered espresso beans. Present from the title company. And they got twice the caffeine as a cup of coffee."

"Sure, why not?" I said. I grabbed a handful and took a seat on the black beanbag chair—sunk down so low my ass hit the ground. So this is what it has come to, I thought, watching particles of cat dander floating about the sunlit room and popping chocolate-covered beans into my mouth like they were nothing. I tried to comfort myself by saying that all new companies started out like this—on hard labor and bootstraps—and that technology was the place to be now. The Information Age had created a whole new gold rush. And with it a belief that everyone could strike it rich. Now every Tom, Dick, and Harry was going into business for himself, trying to be the next dot-com giant. Every day in the papers you'd read about some college dropout who'd just taken a technology company public (working out of his garage no less) and made a million dollars. Some a billion. I had to admit that was partly why I was here. Maybe this little company with its fish-poop smell just might be the next big thing, I thought. It could happen, you know. Me and Bill Gates lunching on crab cakes, co-chairing a symposium on "The Pros and Cons of Internet Cameras in the Classroom." It was definitely something to think about, but not right now.

I didn't feel so good. My heart started racing, and my stomach was doing backflips. Was I nervous about the interview? About making a million bucks? Maybe a little bit, yeah, but I had never been this twitchy before. Something was wrong … terribly wrong. I tried to stand up but couldn't. The beanbag was wrapped all around me, strangling my arms, like it had a life of its own. I panicked. I started wiggling violently, kicking my legs for balance, trying to get up off the damn thing, when this energetic guy in his mid-forties bounded into the room and said, "Who's ready to make a million dollars?"

I froze, legs outstretched, a look of cemented horror on my face. "I am?" I said, currents of electricity still charging through my body.

"Louder!" he shouted. "I can't hear you!"

"I am!"

"WHO?"

"I AM!"

"Beautiful," he said, clapping his hands together hard and bobbing his head like a wired cheerleader. "Just beautiful!" His voice was deep and excited, full of unbridled energy, and his oval brown eyes were wide with the wonder of possibility. It was a look I would later come to know as the classic "techno-geek stare."

It was like they'd all just seen the other side or something, or conquered some new galaxy. Some likened it to the wild eyes of a Vietnam vet who'd been in the bush too long; others compared it to the crazy glow of a coked-out fraternity kid.

Either way, it was scary.

"Shirley," he said. "Hold all calls. I got a man here who wants to make a million bucks."

Hold all calls? Come to think of it, I hadn't heard the phone ring once since I'd been here. Not once. Never a good sign. Not even for a start-up. You remember that.

"Yes, Mr. Plano," she said.

The overzealous geek grabbed me by the arm and yanked me off the beanbag. And before I could regain my balance, he started pumping my hand like a speed freak. "The name's Plano. Skip 'The Chip' Plano. Glad to meet you, Mr. Foster." He didn't look like any mortgage banker I'd ever seen. His dry brown hair was high and unruly, like he'd just been shocked, and he was dressed nattily in a black T-shirt, khaki pants, and hiking boots.

Oh, how I loathed casual Friday.

"Did you get a chance to sample some of those chocolate beans?" he asked. *"Yeah, baby. High octane."*

His face was twitching, my feet were shuffling, and the secretary was busy humming a butchered version of Blondie's "Call Me." I can safely say we'd all had a chance to sample the beans.

"Yeah," I said. "They really hit the spot."

"Super," he said. "Just super. C'mon, pal. Follow me. It's time to make a million dollars."

He led me through a room under construction. No furniture. Just holes in the white walls, chipped plaster on the floor, and rolls of cheap carpet. I didn't know it at the time, but this was a telltale sign, a major red flag. Granted it was a start-up firm, but most companies that intend to pay you properly have the holes in the walls fixed before they interview you. Just keep that in the back of your mind when you encounter such a situation. Anybody that can't afford to fix up their office space, usually can't afford to pay you. It's that simple.

I followed him into his office, hurdling a roll of carpet in the doorway. I was still flying high on caffeine, my stomach making funny noises. *Everyone, please, fasten your seatbelts and prepare for takeoff.*

"Pull up a chair, Mr. Foster," he said. "I'll show you what I'm up to."

I sat down as he positioned himself behind a big glass desk cluttered with expensive computer hardware. The only other piece of furniture in the freshly painted white room (if you could call it that) was a portable blackboard.

"I brought a resume with me," I said, reaching for my briefcase.

"Don't need it," he said, his fingers frantically tickling the keyboard, his wired face glued to the monitor. "You look like a nice guy."

He punched the keyboard, and the monitor flickered to life. "Okay," he said, clapping his hands twice quickly and turning his amphetamine eyes on me. "What I have here, Hudman, will absolutely and unequivocally *blow* your mind."

"Hudson," I said, thinking the Bozo had already blown his mind. "The name's Hudson."

"Yes, well," he said, swiveling his chair toward the computer again. "Whatever. You see. What I have here is a proprietary piece of software that enables me to originate home loans from anywhere in the world. Sound impossible? Far from it. Because, Hudman, no longer will you need to fill out paperwork on a potential borrower. Well, let me stop a moment. I'm getting way ahead of myself. I guess the best way to describe this new technology is to look back at history, then refocus on the future. In the eighteenth century, everyone worked at home, or at least down the street. You had the shoemaker, the carpenter, and the baker. Then, in the nineteenth century, the Industrial Age brought people out of the house and into the factory. But in order to get to the factory, they had to travel. Sometimes a great distance. Thus more machines, more travel-related products, and yada yada yada. Well, as you know, this is no longer efficient in the Information Age. Too many people, and *way* too many cars." He clapped his hands and roared, "BOOM! Then comes the computer. And what has the computer done?"

"Uhhh," I said. "Let us download nudies on the Internet?"

"Yes," he said, "but more importantly it has enabled us to work from home again. It's beautiful. Gorgeous, really." His face was shaking with so much excitement I thought he was going to pop.

"Uh, that's great," I said, "but I still don't know what the hell you're talking about."

"Automation, Mr. Foster. I'm talking about automation. The killer app of the twenty-first century." He abruptly took his eyes off me and smashed the intercom button on his phone. "Shirley. More beans. Bring in the beans."

"Right away, sir," came the hopped-up reply.

Instantly, Shirley thundered into the room with the basket and plopped it on his desk. She then bolted for the door without a word, high-stepping it, her red hair screaming across the room like a tight fireball.

"By the way, Mr. Foster," Plano said, plugging his talk hole with more coffee beans. "You ever step foot into this office again … you're fired."

"Excuse me?"

"You heard me, numbnuts. And the phone? Fuck the phone. It's e-mail only. You ever call me here again … *you're fired*."

I leaned forward, a dumbfounded look on my face. "Pardon my ignorance, Mr. Plano, but I'm not quite sure where this interview is going."

"Of course you don't, Mr. Foster. It's not your fault. Because everything you know about business is obsolete. Paradigms are shifting. As far as you're concerned, the year is now zero."

"Zero?"

"ZERO." His eyes were on fire, and his teeth were clenched tight. "That's because time and space as we know it have changed forever. Let me give you an example." He jumped up from the desk and ran to the blackboard. He then picked up a piece of chalk and started writing furiously. Bits of white broke off as he struck the board, flying like hot sparks across the room. After he finished

writing, he spun around and pointed. "Tell me what you see."

"I see a phone number," I said. It read: "310.555.7319."

"Anything unusual about that phone number?"

"Not that I can see."

"Okay," he said, writing on the board again. "Now tell me what you see?"

I looked at the board and saw the same number. "310-555-7319."

"There's dashes between the digits instead of dots this time," I said.

He smiled. "Your IQ must be well over one-twenty, Mr. Foster, because your answer is absolutely and unequivocally correct. A few years ago, the dots that now separate our phone numbers used to be dashes. January of '95, I believe, was the life-changing event. I know, because I was the individual who created it. I throw this in only because it helps to know the kind of mind you'll be working with. The point is that, when you looked at the number, you found nothing unusual about it. You accepted it. And when America first saw this subtle change, they thought it looked funny. But now, oh, how times have changed. If your business card numbers still have dashes in between, you are looked upon as a relic of the past, a backward-thinking has-been. You see, it's the subtle changes of technology that are changing our lives forever." A rogue smile crossed his face. "The dots, my friend, are only the beginning."

"No offense, Mr. Plano," I said, "but could you please tell me how those dots are going to pay my rent?"

By the way, it is never a good thing when you have to ask this question during an interview.

"Do you have a laptop?" he asked.

"No," I said, still reeling from the whirlwind blather. "I just have an old Macintosh at home. It does a great mail merge."

"Christ, Furster!" he said. "I'm not talking mail merge with a coke machine! I'm talking revolutionary. Your own website. Your own HTML specialist. Video conferencing. The works!" He gave me that crazy apeshit stare, then yelled, "DON'T YOU UNDERSTAND?! People are going bananas over what I've got here, and I'm giving you a ground-floor opportunity. The opportunity of a lifetime to become my number-one beta tester."

"Beta tester?"

He sighed, strolling about the sterile room, combing a nervous hand through his high kinky hair. "I'm sorry, Hadman," he said. "Forgive me for being such an excited fool about all of this, but I find it hard to control my emotions sometimes. Let me see if I can explain it to you in more layman's terms." He bellied up to the blackboard and started drawing a bunch of box-shaped figures connected by lines. "We at First Financial Technologies, or FFT as we prefer to be called, plan to sell financial services online to end users. The boxes that you see here represent the banks, the huge rectangle is us, and the lines are all wires carrying bits of information at dizzying speeds across the planet. Do you know what that means?"

"Sort of."

"It means that we can offer our financial services to anybody over the worldwide web. Anywhere. Anytime. All over the globe. It means taking the customer's loan request over the computer and brokering that information into the financial institution of our choice. They, in turn, close the transaction for us electronically and conveniently wire our commission checks into our designated bank accounts. There's no paperwork. No employees to pay, and no driving on the customer's part. It means, Mr. Foster, that you can conduct your business anywhere in the world—via our virtual office—at double or triple your current productivity." He raised his arms in excitement, his voice arching.

"Can you believe it? And the beautiful thing is I own the software that can make this all happen. Lets the banks talk to each other. That's the key, you know. *Talking.* Because what I have here will eventually put us both out of a job. In time, banks will figure this all out and eliminate the middleman. It's a given in any market economy. And you can bet the competition will be coming hard, too. But … but, Mr. Foster," he said, pointing a stiff finger at me, "there is a window, and we are going to exploit it."

He placed his hands on his hips near the blackboard and bent forward at the waist, staring at me like some evil Bond villain. "But you know what?"

"What?"

"We'll all be *fucking* millionaires by then!"

He laughed out loud and danced about the room. I had to admit it did sound exciting. But one thing still bothered me. How was he going to market this product? You still had to get the customers, didn't you? That takes time and money. And getting customers to sign on the dotted line in any field is no easy task, especially something new and unproved.

"It all sounds great," I said, "but how do I find the clients?"

"Christ, Hidman!" he said, as if I had just offended his digital intelligence. "Are you insane? Word of mouth alone will sell this product. Talk to your family, your friends. Hell, get out there on the street with a sandwich board if you have to and shout out loud, *'I will make your life more efficient! I will make your life richer!'"*

He took a deep breath, looked away for a moment, then trained his mad-scientist gaze back on me.

"They will come, Hidman … oh, how they will come."

All of a sudden I felt the caffeine from those beans giving me one last kick in the chest. I gulped demonstrably and shifted uneasily in my chair, trying to work through it. Plano mistook the discomfort of heartburn for a sign of excitement.

"Look at you," he said, "you're so worked up about this opportunity, you can't even sit still … you're an animal. You want to know about the particulars, don't you?"

He smiled and made a pyramid with his hands, pacing frantically about the room, talking a mile a minute. "Well, for starters you'll need a laptop and an external modem. No less than 56k, of course. Then there's the software that enables us to communicate back and forth, and the two extra phone lines that you'll need installed in your house, just in case we encounter a traffic jam on the Net. Then, of course, there's the monthly subscription fees, employee association dues, and let's not forget about the seminars—"

"How much does all that cost?" I said.

His face went sober. "Not including installation, about six thousand dollars."

"Six grand!"

"I know, I know," he said. "You're freakin'. You're peakin'. But don't fret. Because I just happen to have everything you need right here to join the FFT team. Under our easy monthly installment plan, and I do mean *EZ*, all it will cost you is a low four hundred and thirty dollars per month … and a one-time handling charge of one fifty. That means, for a paltry five hundred and eighty US dollars, this job could be yours, my friend."

He clapped his hands twice and nodded convincingly. "It's a small price to pay for a million dollars, Mr. Hudman. Stock options looming, of course."

"Of course," I said, "but let me get something straight. Is this strictly a commission job?"

"Of course it is," he said. "When was the last time you saw a rich salaried employee?"

"It would be nice to be rich," I said, "but right now I'll settle for comfortable. Rent's due, ya know. Besides, I can't even afford the payment plan. I'm sorry, I—"

"You disappoint me, Hudman," he said. "Do you think I'm shopping for warm bodies here? Do you think I'm offering this opportunity to everybody? Hell, no. This is only for those *special* people looking to go far in life. So what do you say, Mr. Foster? Are you in? Do you got the guts to make a million dollars?"

Picture me freeze-framing this high-haired doofus at the blackboard for a minute, if you will, his big mouth frozen in midsentence. I've picked him for our case study because he's a classic example of some of the huckster salesmen you'll encounter along the new highway of employment. Number one, anytime you hear the word *special* come from a prospective employer's mouth, be sure and substitute the word *fool* for it. Because that's what he or she is looking for. Some fool to spread their gospel for free. I like to call it the free labor movement. It's especially prevalent in start-up companies and those touting ground-floor opportunities. So beware. Because nine times out of ten, when you hear somebody promising ground-floor opportunities, believe me, it's not. You're so damn far off the ground floor by then, your feet are dangling a mile above planet Earth.

These people will woo you with deal-of-the-century excitement, easy money, and the promise of the next big thing. You'll read about it in the classifieds, see a flyer on your car windshield, or grab a take-one at the newspaper dispenser.

"$2,000 PART-TIME, WORKING FROM HOME! $6,000 A WEEK GUARANTEED! RETIRE IN TWO MONTHS! NO BOSS! NO SCHEDULE! NO PAPERWORK! NO SALES PRESENTATIONS! TRAVEL THE WORLD! IT'S EASY! IT'S FAST! IT'S FUN!"

These offers are tempting, damn tempting, because you're so vulnerable after a job loss. And believe me, you'll be thinking you'll just jump right in there and make a million bucks. And then after that, the first thing you're gonna do is pop in on your old boss and tell him to "kiss my ass." But I'm tellin' ya, I'm tellin' ya right now, most of the time it's just a con to make somebody else rich. Not you.

So I'll give you a few pointers on how to spot these knucklehead "opportunities." You can usually identify these hucksters by what they're representing: commission-only sales positions from home, people who don't need to see a resume, shabby office environments that reek of human-rights violations, and above all, expenses paid by you. But the real kicker that should set off the warning klaxons in your head is the employer that you have to purchase something from to get the job, usually in the form of your own marketing materials. Always remember, good employers pay you, not the other way around. That's why they call it a job, dumbass. Otherwise, you're much better off working for yourself.

So don't get suckered in by all the excitement until you've thoroughly checked it out. Because these people are all smooth talkers, highly skilled in the art of exploiting a recently downsized greenhorn. Now, I ain't telling you not to take a chance here, because that one out of ten could be legitimate or right for you. I'm just arming you with the knowledge to spot the crooks and flakes, that's all. Because the last thing I want you to do is waste your time and money when you're hunting for the rent, or God knows, trying to feed a family. (I'm not even going to get into that "We'll pay you to lose weight" scam. I mean, if you're dumb enough to fall for that crap, then you deserve everything you get.)

I remember I learned a lot from that Plano clown because there are a million more out there just like him. And you will meet him along the way, guaranteed. So what I've just told you may not register with you now, because you're probably thinking about sex or something. But one day, you're going to encounter this very individual in your job hunt, and when you do, the recall bells in your head are going to go off like a loud gong. And when you hear them, do yourself a favor.

Run like hell.

-10-

ONE HOUR LATER I was on the phone with Mr. Perfect.

"A start-up commission job," he said. "*No, no, no, no, no!* You definitely can't afford to take that. Not now. You need a guarantee."

"I know, Dad," I said. "I turned him down."

"Just making sure. Any more leads from your friends?"

"Not yet."

"Looks like we're going to have to change the battle plan a little prematurely. Switch to the part-time mode to make it through the holidays. Not to worry though, we're prepared."

"I told you I'm not flippin' burgers at Christmas."

That raised his dander. "You'll flip burgers, you'll shine shoes, you'll put on a goddamned chicken suit if you have to and bark at the local KFC. You will do whatever it takes!" he said. "Do you understand that, Hudson?"

He paused, and I didn't answer. Then he took a deep breath and said with some concern, "You've got to get hungry, son. You've got to get hungry. Did you know that I had to sell my blood just to feed and clothe you and your sister while I worked my way through school? I picked cotton in the fields until my hands bled—"

"I know, Dad, I know. Let's not go there again."

I paced my apartment, feeling guilty for talking back. I didn't want to get into it with him, but sometimes his tone of voice made me so mad I just couldn't help it. Looking back on it, I realize now that it wasn't his tone of voice that bothered me so much. It was the message. A message I still didn't want to hear.

He lowered his voice and said, "I'm on your side, Hudson. I just want what's best for you. But you've got to listen to me. I've been there. Getting ahead is tough in this world, and it's only going to get tougher. It's all about humility and humble pie, and everybody's gonna have to take a bite."

"I know."

"Okay, then. Let's move on. These lectures are killing me. I have the paper here, and I circled a part-time sales job that looks like something you could do in your sleep. It says here it pays twelve dollars an hour and they're hiring immediately for the holiday season. Not too shabby."

"What is it?"

"Home improvement. It says, '*How would you like to earn three thousand dollars by New Year's, selling our services to homeowners nationwide? Comfortable and professional work in a structured environment. Flexible hours. Weekly paychecks and the possibility of full-time employment with benefits. Fax or e-mail your resume.*' You got a pencil?"

"Go ahead."

He read me the number, and I jotted it down. "Sounds good," I said. "I'll fax it over on Monday."

He sighed. "Never put off doing something tomorrow that you can do today."

"Dad, it's almost three o'clock. Everybody's probably gone home for the holiday weekend."

"Fax it over *now*. And then fax me proof that it was done. Just do it, son."

"All right. All right," I said. I wanted to snap back, but I held it in this time.

Later on I faxed over my resume at the local Kinko's, and then I went surfing in Manhattan Beach. It was an unusually hot and dry November evening, and the sunset was orange and red. The Santa Ana winds were blowing in from the desert, and I could hear the noisy cries of seagulls overhead. Sitting there in the glassy water on my board, watching a pod of dolphins swim by, I realized Mr. Perfect was right, *again.*

I wasn't hungry enough yet.

-11-

AT SIX-THIRTY on Monday morning, the phone jostled me from sleep. I answered in a groggy drool.

"Yeah?"

"Hudson Foster?" The guy sounded like a drill instructor.

"You got him, go." How else could I answer?

"The name's Barnes. B.L. Barnes. All US Roofing Company. We received your resume at 1600 hours on twenty-seven November. Quite frankly … we're impressed."

"Thank you," I said, sitting up in bed.

"Hope I didn't wake you. You sound a little sluggish."

"No, no. I just returned from a five-mile run." I gulped down the dry saliva in my throat. "You just caught me with a mouth full of granola is all."

"Outstanding, red team," he said. "You sound just like the kind of man we're looking for. Can you be at the corner of Olympic and Bundy in one hour? Suite 630 in the big glass building?"

"Make it forty-five minutes," I said. "I'm raring to go."

A machine-gun laugh exploded from his mouth. "You got it."

Then he slammed down the phone.

That's one thing I found out about hunting for a job. You never know at what hour one of those type-A employers is gonna call you up and test your mettle. So be ready.

Forty-five minutes later, I found myself sitting in a nice gray suit in a prison-like waiting room full of strangers. The windowless cell was cold and dim, and our simple metal chairs stretched along the east wall. In the center of the square area sat a large oaken table with ten white Styrofoam cups lined across its distressed top. A naked bulb dangled overhead, the room dark with shadows.

I remember feeling a little uneasy at this point. Like I was about to get grilled by the cops or something. *Take me to your leader* popped into my head. I nervously looked around the room, taking note of my fellow job seekers. Not one of them was dressed professionally. The guy to my left had on an actual chicken suit (complete with feathers). The old woman to my right looked like a bag lady, and the rest of the motley crew was made up of pierced and tattooed teenagers in black leather and backward baseball caps.

I kept telling myself that you can't judge a book by its cover and all that other positive crap, but it was still hard to keep from thinking that all these people were born losers. Big Ls in the game of life. The sad part was, at this very moment, I was one of them.

"What are you looking at?" came an agitated voice.

I snapped out of my daydream, still waking up, and realized I was staring at the guy in the chicken suit.

"I, uh, was just admiring your suit," I said. "Yellow's definitely your color."

He leaned over and angrily pressed his beak into my forehead.

"Listen, Mack," he said. "I've got mouths to feed. Six months ago I was right where you are. Nice suit. Fancy shoes ... the whole bit. But look at me now. A friggin' barker at the local Cluck Cluck working for six bucks an hour. But you know what? I need that six bucks an hour. So don't go making judgments about people when you don't know shit."

"I didn't say anything," I said.

"Yeah, but you were thinking it." He pulled his beak off my face, smoothed down his feathers, and took off his chicken head. He looked to be about fifty, an average-looking Joe just like me with a receding hairline.

"Forgive me," he said. "I'm still trying to cope with the anger." He held out a claw. "The name's Hoffman. Peter Hoffman. Harvard MBA grad 1973. Former executive vice president of the Amalgamated Packaging Company. Former six-figure wage earner."

I shook his claw and said, "Hudson Foster. Nice to meet you. And sorry about staring at you like that. I meant no harm."

"Forget it," he said. "You remind me of myself six months ago. Fresh-faced, naive, wearing a suit to these low-class gigs. Holding my head up in arrogance like I didn't deserve to be here. Well, let me tell you something, bub. Sometimes you gotta throw dignity overboard. Sometimes you gotta do what you gotta do. You'll find that out sooner or later. Because everything is bullshit. All bullshit."

"That's a pretty dour way of looking at things," I said.

The chicken laughed. But it was not a happy one. It was the kind of laugh that tried to mask the hurt inside. "Look around this room," he said. "You know what you've got here?"

"What?"

"A group interview, that's what. You know what that means?"

"No."

"It means high turnover. And if you're too stupid to figure out what that means, I'll tell you. It means something is wrong here. It means the company uses people. Or they leave because they can't stand it."

"Then why are you here? Surely an MBA can do better than this."

"You read too many papers, bub. Look at me. I need the bread. I'm fifty-five years old. Obsolete in today's high-tech society."

"But all the economists say unemployment is down around the lows of the early seventies."

"That's because all the economists work for the media. And who owns the media? A few rich fat cats who'll tell you things are good, just so you'll buy more of what they're selling. The press. The politicians. They're all in on it. So don't let their greed lull you into a false sense of security. Most are only trying to make a buck for themselves at your expense."

The chicken man was heavy.

"And you want to know something else?" he said. "If things were that good, why the fuck would I be here?"

I shrugged my shoulders. A point well-taken. He placed his feathered head back on and pressed his beak into my cheek. He said, "You may not have to wear this suit literally, like me. But you're going to have to slip it on figuratively every day. This suit represents the ultimate cold call, my friend. So get used to wearing one. Because you're going to have to bark, scratch, claw, and do whatever it takes to make it out there." He clucked twice for emphasis, then said, "There are no more freebies."

Just then a gruff man in his late forties, with a mustache and a black ponytail, burst through the door with a briefcase in one hand and an hourglass full of sand in the other. He was dressed in army fatigues, and his heavy black eyebrows made him look like a bad guy in films.

"The name's Barnes," he said, setting down his briefcase and hourglass on the table. "B.L. Barnes. But you can call me Sergeant. I served two tours of duty in Vietnam. And yes, I did kill women and children. If anybody's got a problem with that, then haul ass now."

Nobody seemed to have a problem with that. At least, not that I could tell. Probably all too scared to say anything. Just like me.

"Briefly," said the Sergeant, his words coming out of his mouth in rapid fire, "the All US Roofing Company sells its remodeling services to homeowners all across the nation. Home improvement is big business, and, thanks to El Niño and the freaky weather, the industry booked over $115 billion in annual revenues last year. And with the anticipated bad weather from La Niña on its way, we look to have another record season." He started pacing the room, his long black ponytail swinging from side to side. "It's not a hard sell, people, because we have a captive audience, but it does require the art of persuasion. The more persuadables you have in your arsenal, the more money you will make here. The job is all phone work. Inbound and outbound—all leads provided. The pay's twelve bucks an hour, with commission splits over a certain percentage of sales. Some of you might make full-timers, but most of you will be sent home like the pieces of shit you are."

He walked down the line of chairs, eyeballing each of us with a stink eye, his hands folded firmly behind his back. "There are three types of people in this world," he said. "Those that create ... those that sell ... and those that eat shit." He stopped at the old woman beside me, leveled his ungodly gaze upon her, and said in a harsh tone, "My job today is to weed out all those who eat shit." He lingered there for an uncomfortable moment, everybody watching the poor old lady squirm, then took a seat behind the desk.

"You're probably wondering what these empty Styrofoam cups are doing up here, aren't you? Well, I'll tell you. It's your interview. When I call your name, I want you to come up here and pick a cup. Then I want you to sell it to me. Show me your skills. Show me why I should hire a loser like you."

He picked up the small hand-sized hourglass and held it up.

"You got ten seconds to impress me. Otherwise you *di di mau* outta here. You got that?"

We all nodded our heads "yes" as he opened his briefcase and pulled out a resume. He then said, "Mary Robinson, step forward!"

Oh God, I thought. It was the old woman. She was up first. We all watched in stony silence as she slowly stood up and shuffled her rickety body across the cold linoleum floor. She was weighed down by a big black overcoat, and her craggy face was barely visible through a bright red scarf. She stopped at the edge of the desk, hunched, like an old Russian babushka peddling vodka on the street. She said softly, "I am Mary Robinson."

The Sergeant eyeballed her and flashed an evil smile. "Why, old woman, you're as frail as a piece of peanut brittle. What makes you think you can make us money?"

"My resume speaks for itself," she said, her voice rattling with fright.

"I don't give a shit what you did last century, Mary. We're talking today." He picked up the hourglass and turned it over. "Now pick a cup or get out."

The old woman reached out with a shaky right arm and grabbed a cup.

"Sell me!" the Sergeant shouted. "Sell me now! You got ten seconds, you old bag o' bones!"

I felt my blood starting to boil. Nobody deserved to be treated this way, especially an old woman. I was just about to stand up and put a stop to the injustice, but I felt a chicken claw holding my leg down. It was my neighbor. He was looking out for me.

The old woman started to stutter. "This is a-a-a—fine ... cup ... and ..."

The last grain of sand slipped through the hourglass, and the Sergeant smacked the table with his hairy right hand. The loud thump shook her thin frame. "Time's up!" he shouted. "Get her the hell out of here!"

I took a deep breath. I'd always been a fighter for the underdog, and it took everything I had not to stand up and kick that guy's ass. But my neighbor in the chicken suit once again restrained me. The rest of the leather-clad teenagers just sat there stunned, as two orderlies dressed in white coats escorted the elderly woman out of the room.

There was a prison-camp feel in the air now.

"I want you all to take note of that piece of trash," said the Sergeant. "Let that be an example of how not to get this job." He nonchalantly picked up another resume and shouted, "Peter Hoffman! Step forward and pick a cup. Time is money!"

It was the chicken's turn. He took off his head, patted me with a claw on the knee, and said, "Let me show you how it's done." We all watched as the chicken man confidently strutted up to the table, yanked a cup off its top, and shoved it in front of the Sergeant's face. "You see this cup?"

"Yes," said the Sergeant, turning over the hourglass and role-playing along. "It's a cup. *So what?*"

"So what?" said the chicken man, as if he were speaking to a fourteenth-century skeptic. "So what? This is the cup of kings. Laced with gold and silver, extricated from the royal burial grounds of ancient Mesopotamia. It is priceless, said to bring joy and prosperity for all those who drink from its belly. Now you, too, can be its proud owner and experience the magic. And for one day only, the All US Roofing Company is offering you this *incredible* cup at the below-market price of just *ten thousand dollars*. Yes, ten thousand dollars." The chicken man smiled and winked confidently at the gruff interviewer. "Isn't it time you treated yourself like a king today, Sergeant? Now what will it be? Visa or MasterCard?"

The Sergeant smiled as the last granules of sand dropped through the hourglass. "Nice job, chicken. You're hired. Report to personnel tomorrow at 0900 ... but lose the suit. You belong to me now."

The chicken nodded and turned for the door. When he passed by me, he whispered, "Keep your powder dry, Foster."

The Sergeant stood up and said, "That, my friends, was no chicken. That was a tiger. The picture of somebody who wants it. So let our fine-feathered friend be your guide, because he has what it takes to get ahead in this world: the eye of the tiger." The Sergeant sat down and grabbed another resume.

"Hudson Foster! Step forward and show me what you got!"

I'll tell you what. I was inspired by the chicken man's performance. It stirred up something in me that I hadn't felt in a long time. The urge to fight for a steak bone—the will to survive. I stood up and walked tall to the desk, picked up a cup just as the Sergeant overturned the hourglass, and said, "The name's Foster. Hudson Foster. Your wife ordered a case of these cups last week. Where do you want them?" The Sergeant smiled and tapped the top of the desk. I set the cup down. "By the way," I said, "I'm having trouble reading the credit card number she gave me. Can I have it again?"

The Sergeant stood up and started clapping. He said, "The performance of the day, so far. The assumptive close. So all you grunts take note. Because the assumptive close will make you a lot of money in this business." He leveled his hot black eyes back on me. "Outstanding job, Foster. Report to human resources tomorrow at 0900. You're about to get rich."

"Yes, sir," I said.

At that very moment, I forgot all about the craziness, the treatment of the old woman, and the surreal interview methods of a burned-out vet. All I could think about was twelve bucks an hour plus commission. Drinking beers with my buddies and getting on with my life. It's funny how fast you can forget where you came from when the dough starts flowing again.

Just as I was leaving (and I still to this day don't know what compelled me to do it), I turned on my heels and saluted the Sergeant like he was General Patton or something. A real crisp one too. Snapped one off right there in front of all the badly dressed little dweebs. Can you imagine that?

Money. It makes you do nutty things sometimes.

-12-

I DROVE TO Gardner's after the interview. I had to pick up some books. His wife felt bad about giving me that bum lead at First Financial Technologies, so she had taken it upon herself to do everything in her power to get my career back on track. Nice woman, that Max. I told her it wasn't her fault. You have to weed through a lot of interviews until you find something that's right for you. But she wouldn't listen. She insisted on making it up to me. So what did she do? She bought me all these up-to-date self-help books and job-hunting guides. You know the ones I'm talking about. How to get a job in thirty days. How to write a resume. How to dress, act, talk, think, smell, and all that other crap ex-organizational behavior executives are writing about to make themselves rich.

But you know what? Those books didn't help me. In fact, they had just the opposite effect—they screwed me up. After reading all that crap, I became so damn self-conscious I didn't know who the hell I was.

One time I was sitting in this interview, and this blowhard business guy was drilling me with pointed questions. Then he asked me one of the classics.

"Where do you see yourself ten years from now, Mr. Foster?"

Suddenly my mind started racing. Then I froze up. And do you wanna know why? Because of those damn job books! They had me thinking too much. How is my hair? Am I smiling? Am I looking him straight in the eye? My God, I thought, I've got ring around the collar!

So you know what I did next? I didn't answer the guy. That would've been the proper thing to do. I just reached across my body and started scratching the back of my neck like a monkey—speechless—just sittin' there with my stinky armpit in the guy's face. Can you believe that? I didn't say a freakin' word. I just gawked at the man like a dumbstruck chimp and scratched away. Not a care in the world.

"Is there a problem, Mr. Foster?" he asked, looking at me the way a doctor looks at a mental patient.

"Alive," I finally said, still scratching without remorse. "I mean about the ten-year question. I see myself alive."

He rolled his eyes and checked his watch. "That'll be all for today. We'll contact you if we're interested. Thank you for your time."

Job-hunting guides. Flip through at your own risk. Or better yet, just be yourself and keep it simple. You'll get better results that way.

And speaking of results, I was looking for some as I headed up the stairs to Gardner's apartment on that Monday. Storm clouds were moving in. I remember it was cold and windy, and a dense coastal fog was crawling across the street like a plague. Neither Gardner nor his wife expected to be home, so they'd left the door unlocked for me. But when I got to the top of the stairs, I heard loud music coming from within.

The minute I opened the door, I saw Bro Rich posing in the middle of the room with an empty cocktail glass in one hand and a carrot in the other. (You remember him. I talked about him in the first chapter.) He was using the carrot as a microphone, pretending to be a rock star, singing passionately along to Elton John's "Don't Let the Sun Go Down on Me."

He was drunk—out of his gourd, as Gardner liked to say—and watching him sway awkwardly to the music made me want to puke. I didn't like the sap very much, but he was an old friend of Gardner's, so I always tried to be cordial when I saw him. In fact, during the winter of that year, it was something I had to endure more often than I cared to—the sight of him, that is.

The pug-nosed slouch was dressed in his usual preppy attire: wrinkled blue blazer, white sport shirt, khaki slacks, and loafers—no socks. He didn't notice me at first because his eyes were closed. So I just stood there on the threshold a moment, watching the show, taking note of what an idler does on his perpetual day off. He was really getting into it, this guy, his loud, off-key voice hacking the tune, a black forelock of hair dancing across his sloppy face.

This is probably a good time for me to freeze-frame his sorry ass for a minute and tell you a little bit about this guy and why I'm having you meet him. He's a real gem, this one. Somebody you don't want to be like when you grow up. I probably should put a warning label on him—like they do on racy records and TV shows—because I never know what he's going to say or do next. He can be pretty harsh sometimes. You see, he used to be wealthy. But not anymore. That's his problem. He expects too much now. Thinks the world still owes him a living.

His family used to own a big mutual fund company but lost it all because of an insider trading scam. For thirty-one years, he had lived the life of his given name, the finest schools, daily luxury, excessive consumerism, and unbridled capitalism. But now, even in the so-called boom times of the late twentieth century, he found himself penniless and without direction. Most of his so-called friends had abandoned him now that he was flat broke, but not Gardner. His old neighborhood chum had graciously taken him in, in hopes of rekindling his lust for life. In hopes of bringing him back to being a contributing member of society. Instead, what Gardner received that winter was a drunk and a glutton who whined and complained about his fate. He was clearly a man ill-equipped to handle the changing road ahead. A man with a bad attitude who needed fixing to survive.

So let that be a reminder to all of you rich people out there. Wealth can disappear overnight. So don't kid yourself, especially you heirs, because you can lose it all at any time. *Bingo!* Just like that.

I'll tell you a little bit more about Bro Rich as we progress, but first I want us to study his actions and words—learn a little bit more about this creature of pessimism and how you can spot him.

Bro Rich finally looked up after the song ended, focused his beady red eyes on me, and said with a heavy dose of sarcasm, "Ah, Foster. Gardner said you might show up. Something about books." He turned down the stereo and raised his glass. "Care to join me in a little holiday cheer?"

"No thanks," I said, looking at my watch. "It's only eleven a.m. Besides, I start a part-time job tomorrow. I want to be clearheaded."

"Yeah, what's that?"

"It's an inside sales position with a home improvement company. Mostly telemarketing." I shrugged my shoulders. "It's something to tide me over till I get back on my feet."

"A telemarketing job? Christ, Foster. What's next? Buying a futon, moving to Valencia, or shouting '*I got it at Ross*'?"

I always hated the way he talked to me. Real smug—like he was better than me or something. One time he called me a piece of white trash. Said he hated white trash more than he hated minorities. Steelworkers from Fontana. Electricians from Chino. Grease monkeys from Corona. The whole lot of them ought to be taken outside and shot, he'd said. If for nothing else other than enjoying auto racing. Back then I didn't know any better, and I was still letting him get to me, backpedaling on the defensive.

"You wish," I said. "In four weeks I'll have a good job. You'll see. And with my skills it won't take long to get back to vice president status."

He laughed out loud and lumbered over to the kitchen and mixed himself another cocktail.

"Open your eyes, Foster. The traditional corporate ladder is gone. And business titles don't mean shit. Hell, everybody's a vice president today. It's just another way of placating employees seeking a raise. Face it. There's no working from scab to president anymore ... no gold watch at the end of the rainbow. You either start as the president with stock options up the ass, or you start as a grunt and take it up the ass. There's no in-between."

He clinked three ice cubes into the glass. "No, I'm afraid, my naive little friend, the one-dimensional vertical climb has given way to a variety of lateral moves." He chugged his drink and grimaced with defeat. "Most of which are: who's fucking who, who's paying who, and who knows who."

There was an uncomfortable moment of silence between us as we both stared out the window at the darkening skies. There we were, two different people brought together by the economic forces of nature, standing near the end of the millennium, wondering where it had all gone wrong. These were vulgar times, we knew, contradictory times ... times ruled by media obsessed with presidential sex, robust job growth, and a soaring stock market. But nobody was happy. Not even the rich. We were all walking a very thin line. Afraid of the past. Afraid of the future. Because we both knew, at that very moment, that everything we had ever learned about work had changed.

All bets were off now. We were officially free agents.

"So how was your Thanksgiving?" I finally asked, not knowing what else to say.

He frowned, stirring his drink with his forefinger. "You've seen one Big Bird float through the Manhattan skyline, you've seen them all. Yours?"

"Prepackaged turkey. Prepackaged salad. Barry Sanders on the TV." He managed a soft smile, and I followed with, "So, uh, you know where Gardner left those books?"

"Right there." Bro Rich pointed at the books stacked on one of the kitchen chairs.

I walked over and picked them up and took a seat on the red velvet couch, checking out the inspirational titles that would so confuse me later on. Bro Rich took a seat on a purple velvet chair and pulled out a tightly rolled joint.

"Purely for medicinal purposes," he said. He sparked the leaf. "You do understand."

After a series of deep lung pulls, he offered it to me as sort of an afterthought. "Hit?"

"No thanks."

"If you're worried about drug testing, I got some pills that'll mask the THC in your system. They work up to twenty-four hours."

He exhaled and pushed the joint up to my mouth. "Go ahead, take a toke—pee in the cup with confidence."

"No," I said. "I'm not into it anymore. It was just something I tried in college."

I don't know what happened or why it happened, but one day my body told me smoking wasn't cool. Every time I inhaled I hawked up a green loogie. Giblets of some kind. It wasn't real attractive, so I stopped. I'm glad I did. I don't want to end up with some goddamn tube up my nose for the rest of my life.

"You know what your problem is, Foster?" said Bro Rich, holding in the smoke. "You're too optimistic about a future that doesn't exist anymore. Happiness is just a side effect. The world is warming, killer bees are on their way, and the population is graying. We've already seen the best there is. So don't let the six o'clock news fool you, because all they're interested in is ratings. Plain and simple." He pointed at the paintings on the wall, out the window at the approaching storm, then fumbled through the various magazines of style on the coffee table. "Look around, bro. This is as good as it gets."

I finally lost my patience with him. "At least I'm trying," I said. "Not like your fat ass. I mean, why don't you get up off the couch and do a jumping jack or something? Look for a job instead of mooching off your friend Gardner."

Just then Gardner burst through the door with a nine-foot-tall Christmas tree. It was perfect timing. He was outfitted in beige cargo shorts, work boots, and a sweatshirt—his big mane of brown hair tied off with a red bandana. "One of you boys want to give me a hand with this tree?" he said.

Bro Rich sipped his cocktail and said, "Go ahead, Foster, help Paul Bunyan with his catch."

I don't know how Gardner put up with this guy's crap for so long. I really don't. I mean I would've punched his ass out years ago. But that's what made my best friend special. His ability to see beyond the now, his ability to help people who were lost get back on the right track. I couldn't help but think that Christmas that the God of Jobs had gathered us all here in this tiny two-bedroom apartment in Santa Monica to learn about the simple meaning of life. Here was a guy who ran a successful business and had taken time off just to give his time to a couple of bums like us. Hell, he could have been riding around in a Porsche and picking up young chicks if he wanted.

We didn't know it yet, but Gardner already knew something we didn't … the joy of giving.

I hopped up and helped Gardner place the tree in the corner by the window. The heavy sweet smell of pine was fragrant in the room now.

"Thank you, sir," said Gardner, dusting off his hands on his shorts. "Did you find the books okay?"

"Yeah," I said. "Tell your wife thanks."

"The diary, too?"

Bro Rich blurted from the sidelines, "Diary! Christ, Foster, what on earth would you be doing with a diary?"

Gardner came to my defense while fluffing the tree. "I thought it might help Hudson if he recorded his job search. He's always harbored writing aspirations. Now would be a great time to start."

I couldn't have said it better myself.

"Great, Foster," said a tipsy Bro Rich, "the last thing the world needs now is another tale of woe. Another watery memoir from middle-class America, blaming their parents for something they did or didn't do."

"It's not a memoir," I said. "It's just bringing certain things to light."

"You some kind of muckraker, Foster? Is that what you're telling me?" He turned his head toward Gardner. "Hey, G, Foster here thinks he's fucking Upton Sinclair."

Gardner frowned at his alcohol-soaked friend. "Easy, bro."

Bro Rich leaned back in his chair and laughed. "Hell, Foster. You might even get published. *Maybe even win an award.*"

"I'm not looking for an award," I said. "I'm just hoping maybe I can help others along the way, that's all."

"That's good, farm boy," said Bro Rich, "because white male writers don't win awards anymore. They go to immigrants and women and boat people writing Statue of Liberty stories. And all the other heartwarming tales of how-I-learned-to-speak-English-by-watching-*Gilligan's-Island*-reruns." He sighed and sank back into the crushed purple velvet. "Besides, bankers can't write."

"On the contrary," said Gardner, heading for the kitchen. "Bankers and literature have long shared a bed. Raymond Chandler worked in one. So did T.S. Eliot."

"Ah, bull crap," said Bro Rich, waving his hand in dismissal. "Literature is dead anyway. What I'm thinking about is Bangkok. Maybe have a suit made, bang a little foreign snatch." He drained his drink. "Yeah. That's the ticket."

You see what I'm talking about here? Why I'm having you meet this clown Bro Rich. It's his attitude. It stinks. And if you let it rub off on you, it'll bring you down with his sinking ship. Because this is the classic example of a person who has given up, a person who doesn't have the guts to move on, a know-it-all who knows the price of everything but the value of nothing.

People like Bro Rich, or vampires, as I like to call them, specialize in killing self-confidence in other people only because they have none of it themselves. They spew apocalyptic visions, kill ambition, and view all others as beneath them. The insecure ones, like Bro Rich, who were born with money, are the biggest of the negative crusaders. But don't be intimidated by the apparent "class" of these people, because most of them don't know what the word means.

These vampires come in all shapes and sizes and cross all economic boundaries. So be ready when they attack, because it is you, and only you, who will be like Saint George—slayer of dragons—fending off the negative firepower with a positive shield. Because it is you, the one with the smile and the drive and the creativity, who is going to change the world and make it a better place to live—not the idler, the moneyed wastrel, or the apocalyptic armchair quarterback—but you. And only you.

Now, having said that, I want to show you a little bit of Gardner's firepower. How a positive man kicks some negative ass. Up to this point, I've only shown you Gardner the nice guy, lover of nature and man, and all that other crap. But remember, Gardner had a plan for Bro Rich. And it wasn't to come home every day and see him wasted on his couch at 3:00 p.m. watching the Weather Channel. So take note.

After Bro Rich made that Bangkok comment, Gardner went on the offensive. It really pissed him off. I watched him storm into the room with fire in his eyes and knock the cocktail glass out of Bro Rich's hand. Ice cubes went flying. Then Gardner got up in the drunk's face and yelled, "There is no such thing as a free lunch, bro! So get your ass up off the couch and get your roughneckin' clothes on." He smacked Bro Rich's legs with a heavy hand. "We got a house in Malibu to sandbag before this storm hits."

Bro Rich cowered at the powerful force before him and, without a word, went into the bedroom to change, his head hung low. I remember standing there in awe, watching the positive light swirling around my best friend. It was at that instant that I recognized he was someone special. That he had been put on this earth for this very purpose: to help other people help themselves.

"Go on home, Hudson," he said. "I know you probably have some work to do."

I nodded, picked up my books, and left Gardner's apartment. On the drive home, the rain started to fall, and I couldn't help but think that I was pretty darn lucky to have a friend like him. At times I'd taken our friendship for granted. But not anymore. Good friends are hard to come by.

-13-

AT SIX-THIRTY the next morning, the first day of December, thunder and lightning woke me from a strange dream. I was dreaming a lot that nerve-wracked winter, but I remember this one very clearly. I was at one of Mr. Perfect's holiday parties, and this rosy-cheeked guy in a Santa suit was smiling at me from across the room. Then he pointed at his Santa hat, more specifically, the glittery silver letters glued across the base of the white fur.

I think it read: "TINSTAAFL."

I guessed it was some foreign word for Christmas or something—some foreign dude trying to impress the chicks with his knowledge of some language past. Then all of a sudden, he started gesturing at me with his forefinger, wanting me to come over there and see him. That's when I woke up. That's when I always woke up. I would continue to have this dream for the next few weeks, the same scenario playing out over and over in my mind like a broken record. Little did I know I was destined to meet this mysterious stranger at my father's annual Christmas party.

Two hours later—the dream still burning in my mind—I arrived for my first day of work at the All US Roofing Company. The human resources department was a bustle of activity. I counted forty people—all bundled up in their foul-weather gear—in various stages of filling out paperwork in the stark reception area. It had only been a week since I'd been out of a job, but already it felt like a year. While standing in line to check in, I saw the chicken man sitting across the room on a metal bench filling out some forms. He wasn't in his yellow suit. He now wore jeans and tennis shoes and a red vest with the number 30 stenciled in white across his chest. I wondered what that was all about. He glanced up, and we caught eyes and he gave me a friendly chin nod. Then he got back to his paperwork. I smiled, happy to see a familiar face.

When I got to the protective glass window, a large-boned woman with a lantern jaw and silver hair said, "Name?"

"Hudson Foster."

She checked a list and without looking up asked, "Size?"

"Excuse me?"

She held up a red vest and delivered her words flatly, "Extra-large, large, medium, or small?"

"Large," I said. "And if you don't mind, I'd like the number nine. It's my lucky number." Clearly not amused, she shoved a vest under the window with the number 45 on it along with a clipboard.

"Fill out the paperwork and drop it in this slot when you're done," she said. "And, if you like coffee, bring your own coffee mug. The company doesn't provide them for cherries."

"Cherries?"

"Temps … next!"

Nice gal, I remember thinking, putting the vest on over my sweater. Just then the Sergeant entered the crowded room, wearing a headset and fatigues, shouldering his way through a sea of red vests.

"Listen up, people," he said. "It's Howdy Doody time. Time to see what you've got."

I thought I caught a whiff of alcohol on his breath as he passed by me, but that thought was quickly erased as the whole building suddenly shook from thunder and lightning. The lights flickered on and off, and someone screamed.

The Sergeant laughed. "Don't be afraid of that sound, people. Because in this business every storm is your friend." A wicked smile spread across his ruddy, windblown face. "That's the sound of money." He looked up and raised his hands to the ceiling.

"Thank God for El Niño."

The woman next to me was shaking like a leaf, and at the risk of being crude (or sued for sexual harassment) I decided to give her a reassuring shoulder tap and a comforting smile. It seemed to make her feel better. I have to admit, I was a little haired-out myself. I mean, it felt like we were all prisoners in a concentration camp—Christians on the way to the Colosseum.

The Sergeant said, "From now on, you will be known as your number and your number only." He looked at the chicken man and said, "You got that, number thirty?"

The chicken man gave him a steely nod. He looked as ready as anybody.

"It's now time to enter the arena," said the Sergeant. "Just think of yourselves as gladiators, capitalistic warriors, and all you have to do is read the short script that will be sitting on your desk. The leads will be on your computer. The more calls you make, the more money you will make. If you have an equipment malfunction or need assistance, just raise a hand and I'll be there to help. There are two breaks of fifteen minutes each—at ten and three. We'll be the first group in. You'll find your seat by the corresponding number on your cubicle. Please sit patiently for a moment and get comfortable. The part-timers will enter soon after, followed by the full-timers. Then after we have all taken our seats, a brief

introduction by the president will kick off the day's work session."
He crossed his arms and scowled. "At the end of the day, each
person will be evaluated. Those that aren't hacking it will be
eliminated ... are there any questions?"

No questions.

"All right, people," he said, as if leading us into battle. "Let's
lock and load."

We followed the Sergeant single file down a long dark hallway
as thunder and lightning crackled outside. Just then a woman's
tiny voice whispered in my ear, "It's like we're heading for the
torture chamber. I don't like it."

We stopped in the dark for a moment while the Sergeant
creaked open a door at the end of the hall.

Harsh light silhouetted his menacing figure in the frame.

"Let's go," he said, gesturing quickly with his right arm. "Inside.
We got money to make."

I was the eighth person through the door and, when I stepped
into the room, I stopped for a second—staring up in awe at the
mammoth infrastructure of capitalism. The ceiling was two stories
high, and the open room was as big and wide as a football field.
Big-screen TVs and loudspeakers on thick industrial cables dangled
from above, each displaying a different weather report from around
the country. The room itself was as cold as a meat locker and
divided into three separate clusters of cubicles. Over each cluster a
wood sign on chains with blocky black letters identified the ranks:
FULL-TIMERS, PART-TIMERS, and CHERRIES.

But that's not what freaked me out. It was the portrait
paintings hanging on the stark white walls that did that. They
made my skin crawl.

Stepping closer toward the paintings, I noticed that they were
all portraits of the same man. Only it was not a man, but a teenage

boy with a cold smile and a Caesar haircut. The eyes chilled my bones. They were hard and blue—mesmerizing—and they seemed to track my every move. For a moment I just stood there and stared, frozen by the hypnotic gaze.

"Move it, forty-five," said the Sergeant, nudging my arm. "Find your desk."

"Yes, sir," I said.

I stared at the portrait as I walked away, the eyes still following me. I found my desk ten seconds later and settled in. It was your standard cubicle with a phone and a computer. Nothing special. The inside was lined with corkboard and dotted with colorful push pins, and the small trash can that rested at my feet had words stenciled in black across its green belly: "FRAGS HERE." On the desktop was a crisp white script titled: "All US Roofing Company Pitch. Do Not Open Until Instructed."

At about the same time I was wondering when the Sergeant was going to issue us all AK-47s, the part-timers started filing into the room. They wore orange vests and poker faces, and most looked down at the ground when they passed us. The goateed guy seated next to me, number forty-four, peeked his head into my cubicle and whispered, "I heard the kid who runs this place thinks he's a prophet. I just hope he's a good one."

The Sergeant's gnarly voice came over the loudspeakers.

"All rise for the entrance of the full-timers and the president of the All US Roofing Company."

We all rose in unison as Beethoven's "Ode to Joy" kicked in over the loudspeakers. I noticed the part-timers were saluting now, their blank stares fixed on the north wall. Moments later, with the uplifting music playing to a climax, the north wall began parting and the same teenage boy in the portraits stepped through the crack, leading a pack of thirty goose-stepping people in black vests.

He looked just like his picture—a Caesar haircut and metallic blue eyes. But he was much more charismatic in person, I thought. He was upright and lean of carriage at six foot one, and carried himself like a giant killer.

A powerful glow radiated about his hairless face as he glided into the room wearing blue jeans, white sneakers, and love beads over a drab green sweater. But it was not a positive glow, I remember thinking, not the glow you might expect to see around angels, but a glow of death and destruction.

"Holy shit," whispered the goateed guy, leaning in again. "We're working for the beast!"

When the young man reached the center of the room, I turned my gaze upon his followers, the full-timers. They ranged in age, size, and color, but all carried the same hard mean look of a seasoned Nazi. Their shoulders were square, their steps measured, and they entered their tiny cubicles like cult members boarding a spaceship. They did not talk. They did not blink. They just stood there, soulless, staring blankly into idle computer screens, awaiting their next command.

Thought control, I remember thinking. No doubt about it. Big-time Orwell.

We all watched as the teenage boy climbed up a tall wooden ladder positioned strategically in the middle of the room. Then, much to my surprise, he stepped up to the very top rung and puffed out his chest. The music, still playing, grew louder as the young boy looked down upon his flock with open arms. It was clear who was in charge here.

"His name's Julious," whispered the goateed guy. "Rumor has it God spoke to him on a pilgrimage to Jerusalem last year."

"Yeah, what did He say?" I said, unable to resist the juicy gossip.

"Apparently, He told him that the End of Days was near. And that Julious was the chosen one to lead the people to paradise. He's already a millionaire at eighteen. Took the company public in March. He must know somebody up there."

The music died and the room fell silent—all eyes upon the youthful leader. Julious raised his right fist high into the air and nodded down at the Sergeant, who now stood at the base of the ladder. The Sergeant yelled into his headset and it came over the loudspeakers.

"ATTENTION!"

The full-timers snapped rigid like soldiers, followed by the part-timers.

"Cherries!" yelled the Sergeant. "Please join in the ceremonial chant."

For the first time, Julious spoke. And he sounded like a girl. His voice hadn't changed yet. The words from his feminine mouth came slow and soft at first, then picked up steam like a runaway mine train.

"Cash is king ... Cash is king ... Cash IS KING ... CASH IS KING!"

The entire room joined in, screaming the mantra and pumping their fists with passion and purpose. The chant became deafening, grotesque, drowning out the moaning winds outside.

"CASH IS KING! CASH IS KING! CASH IS KING!"

This is insane, I thought. At first I refused to join in. Then the Sergeant noticed my lack of participation and pointed at me with an angry finger. I quickly found myself mouthing the words. It was pretty weird. But I kept thinking about what the chicken man had said, "Sometimes you gotta do what you gotta do."

Ten seconds later, Julious waved off the chant and, in complete silence, climbed down from the ladder. Then, without another word, he was escorted out of the arena like a king.

That's when it all blew up.

A siren went off. Phones started blinking and ringing, and five more headsetted men in army fatigues barged into the room, fanning out like storm troopers. I later learned that these men were called "whipping boys"—their job part cheerleader, part coach, and full-time taskmaster.

I watched these men descend upon the full-timers and part-timers, barking orders and commands and clapping their hands vigorously. The workers responded quickly by placing their headsets on and frantically dialing the phones.

I noticed the TV screens above their heads were showing live footage of the Los Angeles storm, the rain coming down in thick sheets. In an instant, the chatter of the sales pitches became loud and vulgar.

The room was rocking now, buzzing with intense heat.

"All right, cherries," said the Sergeant, standing in the middle of the mayhem. "Listen up, and focus your attention on the big screen above your heads!"

I looked up and saw a sunny rural picture of Middle America.

"What you see on screen is the great city of Little Rock, Arkansas. That's right, people. Bill Clinton country. It looks calm now, but there's a twister expected to hit in three days. And you can bet every hick in town's gonna need a new roof. That's where you come in. It just so happens you have what they need. So open up your script, read it aloud once or twice, and familiarize yourselves. After a few practice runs, dial the first phone number you see on your computer screen and start selling. Any questions, raise a hand. Hit 'em hard, people—and good luck."

Just as he finished, he leaned in and addressed me personally.

"I'm counting on you to hammer them, number forty-five."

He pounded his right fist into his left palm. "Hammer, hammer, hammer."

I smiled and said sarcastically (although I think he thought I was serious), "I prefer to club 'em. How would that be?"

"Oooh, I'd like that," he said. He smiled and smoothed down his thick black mustache. "I think I'm going to like you, forty-five." He walked away and shouted into his headset, "Let me know if you want me to throw more meat on the fire, chief! I got plenty of fresh cherries!"

For the next hour and a half, I found myself talking to a bunch of old Southern ladies. Every one of them had a sob story. Every one of them was broke except for a credit card that was dangerously close to the max. I made two sales, but I felt dirty—like I was swindling people or something. I guess it was the sales script. It bothered me a lot because it was based on fear. The fear of losing your house.

"Hello, Ms. Crabtree?"

"Yes."

"This is Mr. Foster with the All US Roofing Company. We just wanted to let you know that under a no-obligation-to-you drive-by inspection, we found your roof to be in dire need of repair."

"Gracious! I just had a new one put on less than six months ago. Was it you who called?"

"No. Anyway, there's a storm on the way, and you really should get it fixed."

"But I don't have any money."

"We take all major credit cards, ma'am."

"But I don't need a new roof."

This was where the script instructed us to overcome this objection with scare tactics.

"That's what your neighbor said last month, ma'am. Remember the bad rain?"

"Yes."

"Well, your neighbor didn't take our advice, and they're in the poorhouse now. No house left for their grandchildren to play in. You wouldn't want that now, would you?"

"Heavens no, that would be awful."

Going in for the close now.

"I'll tell you what. Since you're on a fixed income, I'll defer your payments for three months. After that it's only two hundred and fifty dollars a month for the next three years. It's a small price to pay for the security of your grandchildren, Ms. Crabtree. Now what will it be? Visa, MasterCard, American Express, or Discover?"

"Ugh. Visa, I suppose."

That's the kinda shit I was doing. Can you believe it? Fleecing old people. I wasn't proud of it. I'll tell you that right now.

At around ten o'clock the siren went off and a voice came over the loudspeakers. "Break time!"

The goateed guy next to me leaned back in his chair, threw off his headset, and rubbed his eyes. He looked tired. "I can't believe I'm here," he said. "Doing this shit for money."

"I know how you feel," I said.

"Do you? I don't think you do. I was making ninety grand six weeks ago selling computer chips. And then this Asian thing hits— bammo! And just like that, I'm gone." He let out a long sigh. "I thought I was invincible, man. I'm only twenty-five. I never thought it would happen to me."

People always think it can't happen to them. But it does. Every day.

He said, "Oh, how I yearn for the good old days when the world was mine and my youthful body was high on drugs." He looked at me with sleepy eyes. "Hey, forty-five. How many sales you got?"

"Two," I said. "But I'm not proud of them. They were two old ladies who couldn't afford it."

"Same here. It's like I'm talking to Abe Lincoln's grandmother on every call. This is bullshit. I mean I really twisted this old bag's arm to get the checkbook. I mean what kind of leads are these?"

"I don't know," I said, taking off my headset. "I really don't know."

I was through talking with the guy. I'd heard him over there working the old people in his Moviefone guy voice, and he sounded like he was enjoying it. I could relate to his sob story about work, but somehow I got the feeling he wasn't being very sincere. Maybe it was because of all the jewelry he was wearing—all these flashy gold chains around his neck and pirate earrings. I hate jewelry on guys. I think it sends the wrong message. The message of easy money and idol worship. But that's just my opinion. Jewelry is for chicks. Period. I mean unless you're a cannibal dancing around a boiling pot of heads or something, it definitely isn't cool. I don't know. Maybe I'm being too judgmental on the subject, but that's how I feel. Besides, the guy was wearing a beeper clipped to his belt. A friggin' beeper! Can you believe that? I mean the last time I checked, the only people who still carried beepers were drug dealers and doctors.

Case closed.

"I'm going to walk around and stretch my legs," I said. "See you in a few."

I strolled over to the soft drink machine and fished out a Diet Coke. I noticed that everyone was going outside on the balcony. Probably smokers, I thought, but the fresh air might do me good. I went outside, and there must have been fifty people huddled together on this one small balcony, smoking and conversing. We were all protected from the driving rain by a large overhang. Some just stared out at the falling showers, others blew in their hands to keep warm. It was a chilly, damp morning, and my bones felt stiff. Stretching my arms, I noticed the full-timers were all clustered together as one unit, their black vests casting a pall over the area. For a moment I listened in on their conversations—sob stories about discount food stores, car troubles, and late mortgages. I leaned on the railing and stared out at the rain, thinking about my own path that had led me here. Probably should've taken the road less traveled, I thought. But who knew?

"For forty days and forty nights a blood-red rain will drench the earth," a brusque voice said. "The first sign that the end is near."

I turned my head and stared into the frightening eyes of a full-timer. He was a portly, big man about my age, with a pocky face and a moppish head of red hair parted in the middle. He looked like the kind of guy who might drive an El Camino.

"Many will die," he said, "but those who survive the free fall into hell will follow Julious to a better world."

I nodded and flashed him a polite smile—hoping the hell he'd go away. He didn't.

"You look skeptical, cherry," he said, lighting a cigarette. "But that's to be expected. I was a nonbeliever just like you, once. You'll come around."

"No, I don't think so," I finally said. "Not the way your boss does business."

"It can't be helped." The big redhead took a deep drag off his cigarette and blew a massive plume of smoke into the chilly damp air. "It is necessary for Julious to amass as much money as possible before Judgment Day. Our people will need it in order to rebuild the New World."

"That's a little self-serving, don't you think?"

"A few must sacrifice for the many," he said. "That's the way it's always been. How do you think every great man in this country has made his fortune? By playing by the rules?"

I chugged the rest of my soda and crushed the can in front of his face. I was hot. "Number one, somebody's got to play by the rules or there would be total chaos," I said. "That's why we make rules. Number two, I don't care enough about money to fuck someone to get it—understand? And number three, I don't give a crap what Julious thinks. He's the devil—a false prophet."

The redhead squared up on me and showed me his true colors, his biblical voice now stripped to the bone.

"Oh, you don't, huh? Then why are you in there, robbing old people of their life savings, Robin Hood? Last time I checked, you robbed from the rich and gave to the poor. Not the other way around."

He puffed his cigarette and blew it in my face.

"What are you talking about?" I said.

"The leads. All cherries do is churn suckers. Every three months, this company changes its name and resells its old clients the same products. Whether they need it or not. It's a scam, but a legal one, if you don't have morals. All you're doing is driving old people further into debt. Taking their last dime and scaring them to death." He turned the heat up on his jaded gaze. "How does it feel to be dirty, cherry?"

I stood there stunned as I heard the harsh sound of a whistle. Then the roar came over the loudspeakers.

"Break time is over! Workers back to your stations!"

The red-haired guy stamped out his cigarette with a steel-toed boot and said, "Go easy on Grandma, cherry." He walked away laughing.

Boy, you can bet, at this point, I was steaming mad. After I found out what I was doing, I knew I had to do something about it—and fast. But what?

Check it out. I was about to blow my top.

When I got back to my cubicle, the goateed guy was busy strapping on his headset. He noticed me and said, "Guess what? You're not going to believe what just happened to me."

I sat down and strapped in. "What's that?" I said, still steamed about the meeting outside.

"I just saw a holy vision of Jesus in the men's bathroom mirror. A part-timer turned me on to the miracle. He's here, forty-five. He's really here!"

I felt my whole body quiver with rage. It was clear to me that Julious was a fraud, just another religious hypocrite hiding behind the shield of God and good. Another Elmer Gantry deceiving the weak for his own pleasure and gain.

"I wouldn't trust what you see or hear in this place," I said. "I smell a rat." (Later on I would find out that I was right. Julious had manufactured those images of Jesus.)

"ONE SALE! You mean to tell me you only got one lousy sale? That's pathetic!"

The entire room fell silent. Then we all looked over toward the ugly voice. It was the Sergeant, and he was yelling at one of the full-timers—an old woman. She had neat brown shoulder-length hair and must have been about sixty years old, I thought. She was reed-thin, polished, and possessed a certain professional dignity that hinted at an earlier life of corporate power and prestige. But not anymore. Like so many others her age, she had lost it all due to market changes in a harsh new world. I could see it in her eyes. She was beaten. Broke. Without savings. Without hope.

"I'm sorry, sir," she said, pleading with the Sergeant, tugging at his army fatigues. "I'm just having an off day. I'll make up for it in the afternoon—I promise. Please, don't fire me."

The Sergeant grabbed the back of her chair and shook it

violently. "An off day! A fuckin' off day! I give you Laguna Beach leads and you have an off day!"

The woman's eyes were wide with fear. Her fragile body rocked in the chair, her spindly arms holding on to the armrest for dear life.

She began to cry. "Please stop, please. I beg of you."

The Sergeant stopped shaking the chair and spat in her face.

"What are you going to do about it, old woman? Huh? Sue me? Sue me for ageism!" He smacked the back of the chair with a heavy right hand. The brute force arched her back. "Who was it that gave your old, tired carcass a shot, huh? Me, that's who."

I couldn't take it anymore. My time had come to unleash. I stood up and yelled, "STOP!"

All eyes were on me, including the Sergeant's. He pointed an angry finger in my direction and screamed, "Sit down, forty-five, or you're fired!"

"Not until you leave her alone," I said.

There were gasps in the room. Evidently no one had ever stood up to the Sergeant before, let alone a cherry. Suddenly a girlie voice came over the loudspeaker.

"There is a cancer in the room, Sergeant … *remove it.*"

It was our little buddy, Julious. I recognized the pubescent voice. No doubt enjoying the show from some undisclosed perch.

The Sergeant slowly walked over toward me on the smooth cement floor and got up in my face.

"Who the fuck do you think you are, cherry? Billy Jack?"

"Just a nice guy, sir."

"Well, you heard what happens to nice guys in this world, didn't you?"

"No. Why don't you tell me?"

He laughed, then poked me in the chest with his index finger.

"They finish last—dead last."

That's when I wiped the smile off his ugly mug. I drove a hard right fist into his gut. It was lightning-quick and punishing, and his drinker's body folded under the force. His body might have been hard once, in the jungles of Vietnam, but it was soft in the middle now. His lungs expelled a wounded groan, and he crumpled to the floor holding his stomach. I stood over him with my right fist cocked, like Ali over Liston, daring him to get up.

"You want to sue me for ageism? Huh? You want to fire me? Huh? C'mon, you piece of shit! GET UP!"

He wasn't going anywhere. He was down for the count. That's when I looked up and yelled into the loudspeakers, "Don't mess with old people! You hear me, Julious? I won't stand for it! I won't have it! Never! You hear me?"

And that goes for you, too. Don't mess with old folks. As you can tell, I'm still pissed off about what happened that day, and I find it very hard to control my emotions when talking about it. We're all gonna meet Father Time, so please show respect for the elderly. Hold the elevator door for the old dude. Help the frail woman with her groceries. 'Cause remember, it's the small gestures in life that make a big difference in this world. And if any of you guys out there ever get any funny ideas about acting the way the Sergeant did, then I swear to God I'll kick your ass too.

When I strutted toward the exit that day, you could hear a pin drop. My head was held high and my shoulders were squared back—everybody staring at me like I was some kind of hero.

Chalk one up for the good guy.

-14-

I WANT TO apologize for that last chapter—for the violence I mean. I don't condone what I did. There are better ways of dealing with bad apples than throwing a punch. Like not working for them, or driving them out of business with your brain. The best way is to not buy their products, especially over the phone. Because it is over the phone where most people get scammed. I know. I was on the other end of the line. I witnessed it.

So I'm going to give you a good rule of thumb to live by when somebody cold-calls you. *Don't buy anything over the phone unless you initiate the call—or you're one hundred percent sure you know who you're dealing with.* Period.

And that includes charities too. If you want to donate, then ask them for their address and phone number. Tell them you'd like to drop off a check in person. If they balk, then you'll know it's a scam. So if you get taken over the phone, then it is your own damn fault. I told you so. And that's all I'm gonna say about that.

My God, I'm starting to sound like Mr. Perfect.

Speaking of him, he was proud of me for taking a stand on that day. I didn't tell him I punched a guy though. He'd probably freak if he heard that. Anyway, luckily, no lawsuits were filed. And I heard they shut down that shady boiler room operation. Evidently my little show of defiance had sparked a revolution.

With all that said and done, you're probably wondering what happened next. Well, as you might have already guessed, I was running out of dough and fast, with no job in sight. After I wrote out my December bills, I had exactly two hundred and forty-two smackers left to my name. You would have thought that the fear of being completely broke would have motivated me even more to put on a chicken suit and start clucking for bucks—banging on doors and shaking hands 24/7. But I didn't do that. In fact, I did just the opposite. I went into my artist phase.

It happens to everyone at some point in their lives, a turning point where you have some time to reflect over where you've been and where you want to go. A point where you say to yourself that you should've been a dancer, a painter, a *Playboy* photographer, or a musician. Me, I wanted to be an actor. Not a leading man because I don't have those chiseled leading man looks. But the nutty neighbor. You know the guy, the guy next door with the self-deprecating humor who gets all the laughs but not the girls. So what did I do? For the next couple of weeks I started not shaving and wearing a Lloyd Dobler long coat around, strolling coolly down the Venice Beach boardwalk at sunset like I was somebody ready to "pop." Ready to be discovered like Lana Turner at a drugstore. (For the record, Mr. Perfect thought I was working on a Christmas tree lot and going on interviews.) Then on Monday the fourteenth it happened. I noticed a handsome green flyer stapled to a telephone pole. It read:

"EXTRA! EXTRA! READ ALL ABOUT IT!
MAKE BIG BUCKS DAILY AS A MOVIE EXTRA!
BECOME A STAR!"

So the next thing you know ole Jed's a millionaire. I quickly hurried home and called the number and, before you could blink an eye, I was sitting in a crowded room with a bunch of wannabe actors, in a dilapidated building off La Cienega Boulevard. It wasn't glamorous at all—definitely not what I'd expected. The room was all musty and dirty with trash on the floor, and the chipped paneled walls were plastered with brightly colored 1950s B-movie posters. (Creature features and busty blondes screaming bloody murder.)

There was a simple desk in the middle of the room, and there must have been fifty of us starstruck dreamers just sittin' there in director's chairs—self-absorbed—all waiting for our "big break." It was a full scene, man. Kind of sad, actually. I felt like a piece of meat ready to be inspected.

"People tell me I look a lot like Jack Lemmon. What do you think?"

The gravelly voice came from the old guy sitting next to me. I glanced over. The only thing that remotely resembled Mr. Lemmon was his clothes—the plaid pants and the yellow golf sweater. Other than that, he looked more like one of those guys who'd been lost in the desert for weeks on end without any food or water. Bilbo Baggins meets Rip Van Winkle. His shoulder-length platinum hair was thick and full, and he had this long snow-white prophet's beard that damn near touched the ground. Instead of shoes he wore a pair of beggar's sandals. (Which I wrote off to millennium madness.) I didn't know what planet this guy had just flown in from, but I decided to humor him. Me being a nice guy and all.

"The resemblance is uncanny," I said.

He flashed me a toothless grin. "You're too nice to be in this business, kiddo. Even if you are a liar." He nudged me with his arm and laughed. The joke was apparently on me. I returned a thin grin and looked away. I was done talking with this moron. Anybody that calls me kiddo automatically gets the cold shoulder. It's just a policy I have.

At that moment, loud disco music was heard coming from the street below. No doubt a lowrider at a red light, I thought. The infectious tune prompted the old guy next to me to start singing along, or trying to anyway.

"I like the good life ... I got to boo-gay ... "

I hate it when people start singing songs when they don't know the words. It bugs the crap out of me. Only thing that bugs me worse than that is a foot-tapper. Or a friggin' whistler. Or a guy who reads street signs out loud. Yeah, any one of them gets my goat. And the funny thing is I never really knew I had a goat until I lost my job. It's funny how the goat just shows up sometimes when you're down on your luck.

I was just about to plant an elbow into the singing guy's ribs when this peroxide blonde burst into the room like a tornado. She was in her late thirties I guessed, tan, and wearing a white sundress with daisies on it. Her red cowboy boots were scuffed, like her smile, and she wasted no time getting to the point.

"So you want to be in pictures, do you?" Her words were bitter and brutal. "You want to fight the cronyism, the payoffs, the casting couch? You want to watch nepotism rise to the top while you, the cream, rot at the bottom like the ill-fated *Titanic*?"

We all watched in startled silence as she took a seat behind the desk, lit a cigar, and blew a thick plume into the stuffy air.

"Well, do you? Then welcome to Tinseltown, honey. Where you're only as good as your looks, your wallet, and your stuff ... in that order, baby." She chomped down on the end of her cigar and leaned back in the chair. "The name's Star. Ima Star. You might want to write that down, because I'm gonna be big someday."

A geek in the back said, "Is that with two Rs?"

"You wish, honey," she said. "One R. Make a note of it and move on." She scanned the room, winced, then said, "Let's make this quick. When I call your name, step up to the desk and hand me your headshot. If you have any special talents, then let me know right away. I'll let you know if I have work for you. And please, no facial gigs or Elvis impersonations."

She picked up a yellow legal pad and yelled in her best game-show voice, "Jesus Rodriguez. Come on down!"

We all watched as a young Hispanic man with a thin mustache approached the woman and handed her his portfolio. "I am Jesus," he said.

She threw her hard brown eyes on him. "You want to be a star, Jesus? You want to be the next Erik Estrada, is that it?"

"That would be nice."

She laughed. "You bet it would, honey. What kind of car you drive?"

"I have my brother's car to-day. Mine is in the shop."

"Well, what kind of car does your brother have *to-day*." She mocked him in a cheap Spanish accent.

"A '59 Chevy."

"Lowrider? Mags? Chrome and stuff?"

"Yes, it is very clean."

"I like clean, Jesus. Can you and that clean car of yours be at the corner of Nordhoff and Sepulveda tonight at nine? In the Valley? They're shooting a Mexican road movie you'd be perfect for."

"Will I have a speaking part?" said Jesus, all excited. "Because I have been taking acting lessons at the UCLA extension. I am very good in love scenes."

"Listen, Jesus. White people don't want to see Mexican love stories. They want bandanas, machismo, and lowriders. So do yourself a favor and stick with what you know—gangbanging and blue velvet."

112

"But that is typecasting."

"No, Jesus. That's entertainment. And if you want to change things, then make your own movie." She scribbled the address and phone number on a piece of paper and held it out to him. "The job's yours if you want it."

Jesus reluctantly grabbed the paper from her hand and walked out with a disgruntled look on his face.

"I don't make the rules here, people!" shouted Ima. "I just enforce them … Sylvester Flanigan. Come on down!"

The old bearded guy next to me got up and went to the desk.

"Do you got any Paul Newman flicks?" he asked, handing her his photographs.

"Not just this moment," she said. She stared at the yellowing picture of a young man in a Hawaiian shirt sipping a beer on the beach. "This isn't you."

"Sure it is," said the old man. "December seventh, nineteen forty-one. Three minutes before the Japs bombed Pearl Harbor. And I got to tell you something, missy. I'm glad I was drunk."

Ima Star sighed. "I'll be honest with you, sir. You do have a look. But all I've got right now are teen flicks. Nothing you'd be right for."

"I can play young."

"What about the beard?"

"It comes and goes."

"I'm sure it does … look, if I got any sword and sorcery pics coming up, I'll let you know."

"I'd make a great Merlin."

"We'll call you," said Ima, shooing him away with a busy right hand.

"Promise."

"No … Hudson Foster! Come on down!"

The old guy's white beard brushed against my shoulder as we

passed each other in the middle of the room. I stepped up to the desk and said, "I'm sorry, but I don't have any pictures. I'm new at this."

"Why are you here, sweetie?"

"I want to be a star. The bread would be nice too."

"Your honesty is refreshing." She puffed on her stogie and exhaled with gusto. "So what can you do? Besides stand there looking stupid with those nondescript cereal-box features of yours."

"I can surf."

"Yeah? But you don't look like a surfer. Not by Hollywood standards anyway. Can you sing, dance, play harmonica?"

This is how powerful the lure of Hollywood stardom can be. I was so caught up in the spotlight of the moment that I started tap-dancing right there. Doing the soft-shoe shuffle in front of a bunch of strangers. Can you believe that? I didn't even know how to tap-dance. Everybody started clapping and hooting, and I started jigging faster and faster like some hick with a jug.

"That'll be enough," said Ima, cracking her first smile of the day.

I stopped, slightly out of breath. "Not bad, huh? Surely you've got something for me."

"Got a tux?"

"Yeah. A little small, but I think it still fits."

"Then you got the job. Be at the Beverly Hills Hotel at five. You'll be playing an upscale dinner guest in a little movie of the week. And shave off those cat whiskers. This ain't a western, honey."

"Yes, ma'am," I said. "You won't regret this."

I pulled the BMW up the driveway of the hotel about four-thirty that same day. It was a freakishly warm afternoon for December, and the area was cluttered with movie trucks, cops, and a bunch of ratty people in grubby clothes all humping cameras and cable. When I stopped the car (expecting to be valeted of course), this cop leaned his head in the window and said, "Extras park on the street, fella. Follow the signs and take the back entrance."

"How do you know I'm not the star?" I asked.

"You don't got the look."

"Yeah? Well you don't look like a cop. How does that grab ya?"

"Move along, sir," he said. "We've got a movie to make."

Friggin' cop. Like he was the director.

Twenty minutes later I strolled into the ballroom wearing a powder-blue tuxedo, shiny black patent-leather shoes and sporting a pencil-thin mustache. (Entrances have always been a strong suit of mine.) The place was packed to the gills with beautiful, chatty women wearing evening gowns and jewels, and the men all looked crisp and dapper in their black tuxedoes and confident smiles. The actual room, or set as they called it in showbiz, was very festive and elegant. Full-on *Gone with the Wind* type shit. There were crystal chandeliers and tables of seafood and a string quartet playing soft classical music.

I gotta tell ya, I was feeling pretty high and mighty about this time, caught up in the phony hoopla of it all. I actually believed I was a guest at a real party. That's when instinct kicked in. I wandered over to a seafood platter and nibbled nonchalantly on a shrimp. Then I surveyed the scene like Clark Gable and winked at a pretty woman across the room. She smiled back. Yes indeed, I thought, if my friends could see me now.

"Hey, buddy. Keep your grubby hands off the food until the scene is over. You got that?"

This little bald guy with thick black glasses and a black turtleneck was in my face.

"Who are you?"

"Extras do not ask questions," he said. "They follow orders." He raised a tiny finger. "And do you know why?"

"Why?"

"Because you're a nobody—that's why." The brash troll walked away before I could smack him. Two seconds later he was standing on top of a dinner table, waving his arms and shouting into a megaphone.

"Attention, people! Attention please! We're behind schedule here, so listen up. We're rolling soon. Obviously it shouldn't be too hard to get into character here. We're all dressed the part ... and just to summarize where we are in the story, our lead, Mimi, has just broken up with her fiancé, Darren, and remember this party was supposed to be in her honor. Now, when she storms through the ballroom crying, I want all of you to have a look of grave concern on your faces. She is the focal point of your attention. Before the entrance, however, I want lots of chitchat, smiles, and false animation. In essence, people, I want big background." He pointed at one of his assistants, a heavyset girl in overalls. "Sarah, put a few extras around the hors d'oeuvre tables."

I was drunk with the prospect of stardom when the big chick grabbed my arm and positioned me at the head of the table. "Feel free to reach for a shrimp," she said. "But don't stuff your face."

"Okay," I said, watching her grab another extra, a long flaxen-haired guy with string bean limbs. He looked like your classic Valley stoner—albeit dressed in a nice tux.

She positioned him next to me and said, "You guys are old friends of the family. When the camera starts rolling, shake hands or nudge his shoulder. Be playful. Talk about the topics of the day and have fun."

We nodded, and she disappeared into the ballroom. The long-haired guy felt the lapel of my blue tux and chuckled. "Nice threads, prom boy."

I laughed. I do have a sense of humor, you know.

"Present from my mom," I said. "What can I say?"

By the way, I'm not going to tell you about my mom right now. That's a whole other story. And it's none of your damn business anyway.

The long-haired guy nodded his head, looked around the room suspiciously, then jammed five shrimp into his mouth.

"The woman said not to eat that much shrimp," I said.

"Screw 'er. I'm getting into character."

"What character is that?"

"The stoned friend of the bride-to-be's little brother."

Makes sense, I thought.

"Besides," he said, "you know how much this little crier costs?"

"Crier?"

"You know," he said, wiping cocktail sauce from his mouth. "Women-in-peril flicks."

"How much?"

"Five mil. So my motto is stick 'em for everything they've got." He inhaled three more shrimp. "And that includes the tux. Screw wardrobe. They cop it all from the Salvation Army anyway."

At that moment, the director, a bear of a man with a beard, in his mid-forties, entered the room like Moses parting the Red Sea. He sat down in a director's chair behind the camera and nodded at the asshole in the black turtleneck. (Who I would later find out was called the assistant director, or AD for short. The whip-crackers on the set. Very seldom do you find a gentle AD.)

"Okay, people!" shouted the AD. "Places! Places!"

All of a sudden the long-haired guy got this serious look in his eyes and squared his body up to mine. The rest of the room was frozen in suspended animation, like robots waiting to come to life. I didn't know what the hell I was doing, or what the hell I was supposed to do. I just stood there looking dumb—hoping for the best.

The assistant director held up a megaphone to his mouth and barked a series of commands. "Quiet on the set please ... quiet ... and roll, please ... rolling ... speed ... annnd ... ACTION!"

The room exploded with laughter, music, and movement, and the long-haired guy was speaking to me like I was his long-lost buddy. "So there I was," he said, "talking to the president of the United States in the White House, the map room to be precise. And he says to me, 'Paul, do you know how many women I've slept with in the past year?' And I say, 'Counting interns?' And he laughs and says, 'Over fifty. That's more dresses than JFK stained in a lifetime.' And then do you want to know what I said next?"

"What? What?" I said, transfixed.

"I say to him, 'Mr. President? I'm hoping you can clear something up for me. Say I'm with this chick. And we agree to take off all our clothes. Then I masturbate over her naked body and eventually ejaculate—her eyes, mind you, admiring the flight of my pearly bullet. *But, but,* nothing ever touches her. Not one drop of semen. Not one ounce of flesh. Nothing. We never even shake hands. Afterward we share a cigar, thank each other, and go our separate ways. Now let me ask you something, Mr. President.'" The long-haired guy put his hands on his hips and cocked his head. "'Did I just have sex?'"

I was really getting into the whole story, so mesmerized, in fact, by his professionalism that I didn't notice the lead actress running into the room crying. Everybody fell silent when they spotted her. Everybody, that is, except me. I just shouted excitedly at the long-haired guy.

"That's insane! The president? ... *C'mon!*"

"*Cut!*" shouted the director. "Do it again!"

The AD yelled at me, "One more slip like that, prom king, and you're gone!"

I nodded sheepishly. While everybody was returning to their marks, the long-haired guy munched on another shrimp and said, "Had you going there, didn't I?"

"You mean you didn't talk with the president?"

"C'mon. I was acting, making conversation for the camera. That's what I do."

"You're pretty good at it," I said.

He smiled. "Two *Seinfelds,* three *X-Files,* and one episode of *Frasier.* And if they ain't enough ..." He paused, looked around the room as if he were ready to divulge enemy secrets, then said proudly, "*Titanic.*"

"*Titanic?* The movie?"

"You see it?"

"Yeah. It was amazing."

"That's because I was in it. Did you see the guys jumping ship when the boat was going down?"

"Yeah."

"Well I was one of them. And if you look real close, you can see me doing a cannonball into the water. It was huge." He laughed like he was high on something. "Talk about big background."

"Places, people! Places!" It was the AD again. Everyone froze.

This time I was prepared for the chitchat, but not the camera.

"Annnd ... ACTION!" called the director.

This is where my memory gets a little foggy. I vaguely recall the long-haired guy talking to me about how he used to be this gung ho Los Angeles Rams fan, until they moved the team to St. Louis, and I also remember a little bit about the actress sobbing on my shoulder when she stormed into the ballroom. (Which the long-haired guy would later call a "nice touch" on her part.) But what comes back to me very clearly was the camera incident. You see, when the star sidled up to me that night, improvising as they say, I couldn't help but notice that the camera lens was right in front of my face. Well, *notice* might be too soft of a word here. Anyway, instead of playing out the scene with this woman like a professional, I stared right into the lens like a deer frozen in headlights. Big eyes. Mouth wide open. Mugging it like some onlooker at a murder scene. But I guess what *really* pissed off the crew was when I actually waved at the lens and smiled. One of the cops outside even said I started soft-shoeing again, breaking into a little *Lord of the Dance*, but I don't remember it. Swear to God, I don't. It was like I was under a spell or something.

"CUT! LOSE THE GUY IN BLUE!"

Those were the last words I heard as two beefy grips physically removed me from the set and tossed me outside. The sky was fiery red, and all I could think about was Homer in *The Day of the Locust*. I also remember thinking it was official. My dreams of Hollywood stardom were over—gone forever. It took me a long time to get over that night. Only because I really thought I was going to be somebody. That it was my destiny to become a star, a household name around the world. That's what drives most of us, at first, toward the glamour fields, I think. The prospect of being somebody rich and famous. The hope that one day you'll return to the old neighborhood in a big black limousine shouting, "Hey, look at me! I hit it big!"

Well, let me tell you. Making it in showbiz is a lot tougher than that. It's about hard work, talent, luck (lots of luck), perseverance, and dedication. But more importantly it's about *who* you know. So I'm gonna give it to ya straight. Because that's just the kind of guy

I am. Most of you will never make it in Hollywood. That's because the deck's stacked against you. It's just like Vegas in that respect. It's one big gamble. You see, Hollywood likes to grow its own. And they like to keep it all in the family—from cradle to grave. Sheer will and determination don't always ensure success as an actor, writer, director, or producer. Not like they do in other walks of life. For the most part it is a closed society, the plum assignments going only to those with the money or the pedigree. That's just the way it is. So, if you're lucky, you'll go on to work behind the scenes, become a teamster with an embroidered jacket, or a desk jockey in the marketing department of a studio. Oh, you'll still have the malt shop discoveries of course, the rare overnight sensations, but this type of fame rarely lasts. Most discoveries are based on looks and age alone. But that kind of fame eventually fades (or sags) depending on your situation.

But don't let anything I've said up to this point deter you from chasing your dream. Hollywood needs fresh souls—I mean fresh faces—every day. Just be prepared for failure as well as success. And if you want to be in the entertainment field, then you'd better be prepared to put up with a lot of crap—and a ton of rejection. On the way to the top, you'll have to wade through some of the sleaziest characters you've ever met in your life. That's because fame and fortune bring out the worst in people.

Druggies, posers, mobsters, flesh peddlers, and flimflam artists—they're all crawling in Hollywood. Especially the bitter, pinched types like Ima Star, who have finally realized that, after age thirty, their dreams of Hollywood stardom are nothing more than a memory. They're easy to spot out there. Operating on the fringes of the business, they spew bitter, jealous words aimed at fresh-faced newcomers who still have a shot at making it. They don't like their jobs, and they don't like you. But don't let them derail you. There are a lot of good people out there, too. You just have to know where to look. Be patient, check references, and you'll do all right.

So what happens if you've given it your best shot in Hollywood and you still haven't "made it"? That's the million-dollar question for most artists. Knowing when to hold 'em and when to fold them. Knowing when it's time to give up on a dream and move on. All I can tell you is you'll know. You'll know because it isn't fun anymore. You'll know because you can't make a living at it. You'll know because the business or your family will tell you it's time. It will be a difficult realization in your life. But you'll get past it. There are other dreams, you know—other moments. And to those people who truly gave it their best shot out there in Hollywood before throwing in the towel, I say this to you: Put all that positive creative energy back into the community. Write a poem. Produce a local play. Teach a class. And who knows? If you forget about fame and fortune for a while, you just might find out that the art in your life is what people really care about. Never stop dreaming. Because recognition always finds the truth.

And for those lucky few who do make it (and it might be you), cherish it for the art. Not for the fame and fortune, but for the art. Make us laugh. Make us cry. And don't hold nothin' back. Because you're one of the lucky ones. So enjoy it. Just don't give us that star bullshit. I'm tired of all that tabloid crap. It wastes too much paper. Always remember you put your pants on one leg at a time, just like the rest of us. You do that and you'll go far. I swear you will. So when you're up there sniveling with the Oscar or Emmy in hand, all decked out in your best designer clothes, be sure and thank your good buddy Hudson Foster for keeping you grounded—for giving you the inspiration and information.

Even a knucklehead like me needs a little recognition once in a while. It's just human nature.

-15-

I NEVER TOLD Mr. Perfect about my trip to Hollywood. All that would have produced was another I-told-you-so. And who needed to hear that when I was down on my luck—down to my last one hundred dollars and sinking fast? It has been said that God never gives anyone more than they can handle. I was hoping that was true now. I did find out something new about myself during this bleak time, though. I liked to write. It made me feel better. And you know what? The more I did it, the better I got.

So before I push on, I'd like to share some of my diary entries with you. I think you'll get a kick out of them.

Hudson's Log: Stardate 15 December

The Gardners invited me over for dinner tonight. Meatloaf and broccoli. Afterward we all watched old movies on TV. *White Christmas* and *The Sound of Music*. I wasn't in the mood to watch either one, but I guess it could've been worse. I could've been shackled to a medieval stretch rack and forced to watch *Dances with Wolves*. We settled for Julie Andrews. I think I spotted a crotch-shot spinning in the meadow, but I'm not sure. Gardner could see I was pretty down, so he started giving me his usual pep talk about being the ball and all that other crap. About how faith and the new Age of Aquarius would prevail in the new century. I have to admit I wasn't listening very much. At least I wasn't until he said he gave Bro Rich a job at his furniture factory. I don't know why, but deep down I felt betrayed. Why hadn't he offered me a job? Couldn't he see I was desperate? I don't know. Maybe it's not always a good thing to work for your best friend. I guess that's what he thought anyway.

Hudson's Log: Stardate 16 December

High noon. I sit in my apartment in a pair of sweatpants, drinking vodka from a wineglass. A hard winter rain falls outside. On the news, strong waves hammer beach houses, seals wash ashore, and traffic accidents litter the wet roads. I read through the want ads looking for a job. I wonder why they don't have a section for Guys? They do for Gals, sandwiched right between Fundraising and General Office. I think about becoming a gigolo. Easy money, credit cards, and stretched-out Beverly Hills divorcees. The thought quickly passes. Who am I kidding? I'm no Tom Cruise. I've gotta face shaped like an anvil.

Hudson's Log: Stardate 17 December

I had the dream again last night. The same dream about the rosy-cheeked guy with the TINSTAAFL hat at Mr. Perfect's Christmas party. I guess I'll find out soon enough if I've got Edgar Cayce powers, or if I'm just another nut job from L.A. My father's party is only seven days away now. Hopefully I'll have it all figured out by then. I also had dinner with Gardner and his wife tonight— KFC extra crispy. I noticed a couple of Christmas lights burned out on their tree, but I didn't say anything. Just stared at the model train going round and round. After dinner we all watched one of those animal shows on the Discovery Channel. It focused on a watering hole in the Serengeti Plains. When this nervous zebra tried to snatch a quick drink from the water's edge, this nasty crocodile bit him in the ass. The poor animal let out a death groan. I know how he felt. Gardner's wife couldn't bear to watch anymore, and she ran out of the room screaming. It was my cue to bail. So much for 'tis the season.

As you can tell, I was really starting to get down on myself, wondering why the world had it in for me. I mean, it was like God had issued me my own personal black cloud or something. *Follow that man and rain down on his parade every chance you get. We have it in for him.*

And since the world had it in for me, I decided to return the favor. I started roaming the streets with that nine-bucks-left-in-my-checking-account look. My face desperate. My mood uncivilized.

I went into the grocery store and made a scene over an apple, thinking I could haggle my way through anything. *"You gotta be kiddin' me! Fifty cents for this bruised piece of crap? C'mon! I'll give you a dime and not a nickel more."*

I left the store empty-handed. Worse yet, I had to duck the Salvation Army lady on my way out. I got good at that. Duckin' those bell ringers. I mean, the minute I heard that damn bell ring, it was like Pavlov's dog. My hands dove for my pants pockets—viciously protecting what little change I had left—my head went down, and I walked right on past that do-gooder with passion and purpose. "Sorry," I mumbled through the night air. "I already gave at the office."

I'm giving you this sad bit of information for a reason, so you can recognize it when it starts happening to you. The world doesn't have it in for you. It just seems that way. You're down. You're beaten. You're broke, and you don't want to get up and face another day of rejection. I know I didn't. So what did I do? I did what a lot of us do when we don't want to face the world anymore. I shut it out. I holed up in my apartment, eating junk food and watching daytime TV in my sweatpants.

Ding Dongs. Twinkies. Fruit Loops. Bring it on! YEAH! Because I deserve to get fat! I deserve everything I get because I'm a big fat loser and I had it all coming to me. Well, of course I didn't (and you usually don't either), but at that stage of the game, I was too blind to recognize it. You will be too. And that, my friends, is when you are at your most vulnerable to the dreaded pitchmen on TV. The sleazy gurus who prey on us out-of-work people to make themselves rich.

"Are you tired of living paycheck to paycheck? Are you tired of working for people who lack vision? Tell me, are you ready to make a change in your life today? Then yes, folks, maybe it's time to take control of your destiny and enter the fascinating world of no-money-down real estate. In just three short days you'll learn all you need to know from my tapes to become the next tycoon on your block. So pick up the phone and order today. Only twelve easy installment payments. And if you act now, I'll throw in 'How to Hypnotize Your Escrow Officer' at no extra charge ..."

So I acted. Falling for what I call blockbusteritis, or "get rich quick" schemes. Because if there's one thing we humans like more than making a lot of money, it's making a lot of money *fast*. Blockbusteritis usually occurs when you've hit rock bottom—when you are *this close* to becoming one of those guys you see on the beach wearing headphones, a beer-can hat, and hunting for pennies with a metal detector.

It happens to all of us. So I'm going to give you a little bit of information on how to spot these traps. The most recognizable, of course, is the guru. And how do you spot the guru? Easy. It's the smiling guy who's always got his picture plastered on his ads or his corporate walls. (Remember Julious?) Or the clown in the infomercial, sailing his yacht around and sipping cocktails with two young chippies draped around his body.

Testimonials are another way to spot these frauds. You know, the glowing recommendations received from supposed punch-drunk customers. *"Hudson Foster made me one billion dollars in just three short days!"* ... *"If it wasn't for Mr. Foster's methods, I'd still be driving a big rig in Omaha."* ... *"Mr. Foster truly changed my life."*

But the crazy thing is we still buy, don't we? Why? Because these gurus are really slick, I tell ya. Some of them even hire a bunch of washed-up celebrity pitchmen to hawk their wares. That's what happened to me. One of my favorite football stars suckered me into some golf scam. The bastard. And for what? Money ... money for the guru.

So anytime you see way too many pictures of someone selling something, or an aging celebrity, beware. 'Cause that smile you see just might be fake. Oh, and before I move on, I just want to mention the mail and the phone calls you seem to fall for when you really need the dough. The opportunities you usually ignore when you've got a job. I started getting all these sweepstakes offers in the mail telling me I'd won millions of dollars. You know the ones: *"Hudson Foster has just won 10,000,000 dollars!"* Of course I never read the fine print—and I didn't win ten million dollars. It was just a come-on to get me to order some product or send money. That's how they get you. You either call a number that costs you money, or you send in a small dollar amount to "claim" your winnings—for administrative fees or some shit. Oh, I'm not bagging on any of the legitimate contests. The ones with the famous dudes who knock on your door. But don't be fooled by them either. Those same bastards are jiggling your millionaire chain just like the rest of them—making you think you gotta order magazines to win. You find yourself ordering *Squirrel Fancy* or *Drywall Illustrated,* or some other piece of literature you wouldn't even use to spank your dog. Besides, after seeing the winners on TV, I noticed something. People in apartments rarely win, if ever. It's always the little house on the prairie with rolling meadows and big oak trees that they're knockin' on. Think about it. When was the last time you saw the prize patrol in the ghetto?

My point is if it seems too good to be true, it is. So use common sense and don't get suckered in by all the pictures of Learjets, fast cars, and people with model looks playing golf in Hawaii. It's a scam. It has always been a scam, and it always will be a scam. Bottom line. You don't get something for free—especially from people you don't know. So don't waste your energy unless you've got a negotiable bank check in hand. I learned that one the hard way during my unemployed days. Of course, I would've never known any of this stuff if it weren't for Mr. Perfect. If it weren't for him, I probably would've turned into one of those guys who tries to earn a living by playing radio contests all day. You know the people. Three radios blaring at once. Three phone lines and headsets going—listening intently and shit for some Mariah Carey song—praying. Just praying to God you're caller number ten.

"I'm sorry, sir, you're caller number eight."

"Dammit! This freakin' close!"

It was Mr. Perfect who rescued me that day from all the charlatans. Although at the time I thought he was just about the biggest jerk I'd ever known. So here's the scene. There I was, on a chilly gray Thursday afternoon, wallowing in my own self-pity, feet propped up on the couch, body swimming in guru tapes and marketing materials, orange Cheetos mix smeared all over my face, when suddenly the door burst open. And there he was. Bigger than life. Standing in the doorway with his huge arms crossed, wearing a long blue raincoat, his famous granite chin jutting out like the Rock of Gibraltar. No doubt about it. It was John L. Foster. Mr. Perfect himself.

"What are you doing?" he said.

"Uh," I said, with a look of stupid surprise on my face. "I was just about to pop this motivational tape into the VCR, Dad."

He didn't buy it.

"Is that Oprah on the TV?"

"What?"

"You want to be a bum for the rest of your life, Hudson? Is that it? You want to wear sweatpants to work? Okay, smart guy. If you don't want to look for a job, then I'm going to put you to work. For the next few days you're mine—eight to five."

I sat up, stunned. "What will I be doing?"

"Chores."

Picture me with one of those soap-opera looks on my face and dramatic classical music mushrooming in the background. "Chores?"

Mr. Perfect strutted into the middle of the messy room. "You'll start by washing my car and detailing it. After that, it's grocery shopping. You'll get one hour for lunch, then it's back to cold-calling prospective employers. I'll monitor your progress with a flow chart."

There comes a time in every man's life when he thinks he can finally kick his father's ass. The day he says to himself he no longer has to take this shit. This was not that day. Even though my father was fifty-seven years old, he was still in great shape. (Probably from all those morning workouts with Jack LaLanne and that goofy ab roller under his bed.) He was tall at six foot four and muscular with salt-and-pepper hair, and he had the resolve of a pit bull fighting over a steak bone. Why he was taller than me, I don't know. Most of my friends were taller than their parents, but not me. It was as if my father had purposefully denied me this genetic code.

The last thing my father said to me that day was, "I'll see you tomorrow morning at eight. And get a haircut. I want you looking presentable for the Christmas party." Then he disappeared out the door with his dark shadow.

"Slave driver!" I yelled, shaking my fists in the air. "Fascist Commie bastard!"

-16-

THE NEXT FOUR days were hell. Mr. Perfect had me scrubbing toilets, washing cars, and doing his grocery shopping. Which was an adventure all unto itself, let me tell ya. Hanging out in the frozen food section counting calories with a bunch of stressed-out soccer moms was not my idea of a good time. And when I brought home the wrong Lean Cuisine dinner? Forget about it. He freaked. Said he didn't like the sauce on this one. The onions on that one. And how could I have picked the baked fish over the chicken oriental? *Stupid. Stupid.* He also told me that it was my lack of attention to details that landed me where I am today. But you know what? After everything was said and done, Mr. Perfect's little plan actually worked. After a nightmare round of daily chores, I was glad to get back on the phone and start cold-calling prospective employers—happy to dust off the chicken suit and start clucking again.

It didn't take me long to snag an interview either. I got one on the last Tuesday before Christmas. It was for a loan officer position with one of the state's leading financial institutions. I was back, baby. Or so I thought.

Now, I want you to pay close attention here. This is a very big chapter. A lot of shit goes down in this chapter. Which reminds me. I know people are supposed to change for the better toward the end of novels, so in keeping with tradition, I'm going to change too—or go through some kind of character arc, as they say in the movie business. You ready? I'm not going to cuss anymore. That's right. Not because I have to, but because I want to. After hearing bad words spew from other people's mouths for so long, I've noticed how ugly it really sounds. And if I can do my part to clean up some of the noise pollution in these vulgar times, then that's a good thing, I think. I'm still working on my temper, though. So I can't promise you anything there. But I'm not going to use bad words anymore. I swear! And when Hudson Foster makes a promise, by God, he sticks by it.

Now that you know that, I want you to take a trip with me back in time to that fateful Tuesday when I interviewed with the infamous Mike Skull, executive vice president of America's Favorite Bank. He's our next case study. And he's a real gem—so listen up.

I arrived at the corporate headquarters of America's Favorite Bank wearing my presidential blue power suit. It was about nine in the morning, and the sun was soft and golden in the pale blue sky, the air crisp and clean. I remember standing outside in front of the big glass building, admiring my reflection in the window. I was anxious to get back on the fast track again—anxious to sharpen my executive pencil. *How about some coffee, Mr. Foster? ... Mr. Foster will be with you in a moment ... Sure thing, Mr. Foster, anything you say.* I guess the real reason I was happy to be back in a suit again was the money. The only money I had ever really earned in my entire life was made in a suit. To me a suit represented a living, but more than that, wealth and power.

My interview was at nine-thirty, but, as usual, I had arrived early to find a free parking place. But there is one other reason for arriving early that I forgot to tell you about. You might need to go to the bathroom. I learned that one the hard way, too. You see, one of the things that gets all thrown out of whack when your routine changes is your body clock. Not to mention you get real nervous when you're this far down in the job-hunting game. One time I was having an interview with this important firm at eight-thirty in the morning (which is my normal bowel movement time), listening to this guy ask me what I wanted to do with the rest of my life, when all of a sudden I started percolating. I mean really percolating. I'm talking pasta and bread for dinner the night before. Well, of course I had no choice but to excuse myself by rudely cutting the guy off and saying, "Hold that thought." Then I sprinted out of the room, slightly hunched, did my duty, and when I returned from the bathroom, he was gone—along with the opportunity. So allot some bathroom time for yourself before your interview. But never use the bathroom on the same floor your interview is on. You don't want to take a chance of running into the big cheese. Meeting someone after you've just pinched one off is never a good thing. Nobody wants to shake your hand.

So at 9:29 a.m., after using the seventh-floor bathroom to "freshen up," I took the elevator to the ninth floor—the floor my interview was on. Striding down the hallway, I was the perfect picture of class, confidence, and poise. My hands were close to my sides, and my hair was perfect. And do you want to know why? Because Big Brother was probably watching—that's why. With the recent technological boom, all these big companies have tricked out their headquarters with hidden cameras and microphones. So my advice to you is to look straight ahead and smile when you're inside the building, especially in elevators and hallways. Don't pick your nose or scratch your butt. Because you never know when some sap is watching you from a hidden bank of monitors or from some satellite up in space. This may sound paranoid, but you know what? It's a real threat, and it might cost you. I don't like what's happening to my privacy in the workplace any more than you do. That's why I'm passing along this information. Expect to be watched, and you won't give anything away.

At nine-thirty sharp, I stopped at a large oaken door marked with gold letters. It read: "HUMAN RESOURCES." I took a deep breath, cracked my neck, mentally put on the chicken suit, and walked in. I was immediately greeted by a pleasant young woman at the reception desk, with long honey hair and reading glasses. "May I help you?" she asked.

"My name is Hudson Foster. I have a nine-thirty with Mike Skull."

She smiled like an angel. "One moment, please." She picked up the receiver and, after a brief conversation, said, "He'll be with you in a minute, Mr. Foster. Please have a seat."

"Thanks," I said, soaking up the sweetness of her perfume. I walked across the plush carpet and took a seat on a cream-colored couch. It was a beautiful office suite, I noticed. Expensive paintings on the wall, fresh flowers on the coffee table, antique furniture, and up-to-date magazines. I gotta tell you it felt good to be back in the big leagues again. No more boiler room operations, no more infected phones, no more nose rings or movie people in blazers and T-shirts. But most of all, no more toilets. Although I will tell you this. Working all those "menial" jobs for Mr. Perfect made me appreciate how hard those people work who do them for a living. I've got a lot more respect for those people now.

"Hudson Foster?" The voice I heard was a smooth Southern drawl. When I looked up, I saw a polished executive standing before me in a hard gray suit. He had a prominent forehead, a crew cut of brown hair, and a backwoods smile borrowed from *The Texas Chainsaw Massacre*.

"Yes," I said, rising up from the couch.

"Mike Skull. Vice president of recruiting for America's Favorite Bank. Nice to meet you." We shook hands vigorously, eyes locked.

"Nice to meet you, too," I said, looking around now. "This sure is a beautiful office."

Small talk. Always remember the small talk.

"Yes indeed," he said. "We have some pretty fancy interior decorators that keep us knee-deep in style out here." He smiled. "Know what I mean?"

"Yeah," I said, impressed. "It's nice."

"C'mon back, Hudson. We can talk in the conference room." I followed him into the office area, noticing my fair share of beautiful ladies along the way. But I quickly shook all thoughts of sex from my head and refocused on getting the job. I was here for one reason and one reason only: money. So when I walked through the conference room door, I had the look of a German luger getting ready for a gold medal run in the Olympics. Adrenaline on high. Chicken suit times two.

"Have a seat," Mike Skull said, "and relax."

Maybe I was a little too focused. I smiled and vowed to just be myself. We both sat down. It was a big conference room with state-of-the-art equipment. We sat at opposite ends of the long table. I waited patiently as Mike Skull reacquainted himself with my resume.

"Too bad about the merger at Frontier," he said, staring at the paper. "It came as quite a shock to corporate here."

"Me too," I said with a wry smile, my hands fidgeting underneath the table.

He laughed, stopped abruptly, then stared at me like Walker, Texas Ranger. "Married?"

"No."

"Good. Old politics used to favor marrieds. The reasoning was they'd work harder if they had a family to feed. Not anymore. Families are anchors now. They want too much money and way too much time off. If a business is to survive in the new global economy, then it's got to be lean and mean. It's a fact of life, Mr. Foster. Profit margins are shrinking, and the population is growing. That means more competition. Which means longer hours for less pay. But for a young guy like you, it means opportunity." His tough-guy look grew harder. "Are you prepared to work nights and weekends when we need it?"

"Absolutely," I said. "Whatever it takes."

"Good. You a whiner?"

"Excuse me?"

"A lawsuit hound. One of those employees who's ready to sue at the drop of a hat."

"I'm old school," I said. "I don't believe in suing. You won't have a problem with me."

"I didn't think so," he said. "But I had to ask it. Just in case you planned on hopping aboard the sexual harassment bandwagon."

"I'm far away from that bandwagon, sir."

"Good. If you ask me, all those women who sue their employers for sexual harassment are only hurting themselves. That's why I don't hire many skirts anymore. Why take a chance when you can hire a man? Men rarely file those kinds of suits. I mean, what's the world coming to when you can't play a little grab-ass in the office once in a while?" He smiled like a hillbilly. "Know what I mean?"

"I know what you mean, sir," I said. I didn't, but what else could I say?

"Shoot," said Mike Skull, scratching his extra-large forehead, "I'd love it if some broad grabbed me by the balls over by the water cooler and told me I had a pair. Wouldn't that be great?"

"I know I'd look forward to going into work every day," I said.

"You bet you would, boy. Do you speak any languages?"

"Yes."

"How many?"

"Two."

"And those would be?"

"English and 7-Eleven."

This cracked him up. He pointed his finger at me and said, "I like that. That's funny. A good sense of humor in a man is a sign of strong character." He leaned back in his chair and folded his arms. "You're probably wondering where I'm going with all this superfluous questioning."

As a matter of fact, I did.

"Well I'll tell you," he said. "America's Favorite Bank, or AFB as we like to call ourselves, answers to one group of people, and one group of people only—"

I chimed in with what I thought was a no-brainer. "Its customers?"

"Heck no," he said, stunned. "Its board members. We keep them happy, and I keep you happy. Because we at AFB are all about the bottom line. To be honest with you, Hudson, we don't give a rat's patootie about the customer anymore. Pardon the French. It's all about fee income today. And the only way you can generate more fee income is by monopolizing an industry. And with more and more immigrants coming into the country, and the average Joe getting dumber by the day, we see a huge opportunity with the masses. When the customer has only one bank in the neighborhood to visit, then you got them by the balls." He held out his right hand and made a squeezing gesture. "You don't ask for the business anymore, Mr. Foster, you take it."

"I see," I said. "Does AFB have a specific marketing plan in place to achieve its goals?" This is the kind of generic question that employers love to hear. It's *proactive.*

"Good question, son," he said. "And the answer is yes. In the next ten years, we intend to drive out every local mom-and-pop bank in the country. Put 'em all out of business." He smiled. "Size does matter."

"Sounds ambitious," I said. "But a little risky, don't you think? I mean, look at Japan. They are the perfect example of how an economy can topple under the bigger-is-better theory."

"True," he said. "But the sushi boys got greedy. Too many bad loans. Too many incestuous relationships. And when that happens, payola and kickbacks rule the bottom line. We don't intend to make that same mistake here, Mr. Foster. Besides, when you own every money machine in the country, there's plenty of cash to go around." A lecherous smile crossed his face. "If you want customer service, partner, use the ATM."

I could've debated economics with him all day, but the truth of the matter was I was wearing dirty underwear and socks (laundry money had been sadly replaced by another necessity on that day: gasoline), and I was eager to get on with my life—such as it was.

"It sounds like you'll be fully automated in regards to deposits," I said, "but with all due respect, Mr. Skull, could we please discuss the loan officer position in a little more detail?"

"An eager beaver, are ya? Well, for starters, how does an 800 number campaign sound? Home loan approval in *five* minutes."

"Sounds great," I said, "but what about your interest rates? If they're not priced competitively, you'll be spinning your wheels. Rates are at thirty-year lows."

"Son, when you're the only game in town, *who gives a hoot about rates?* You must understand we're selling convenience here. Not product."

"At above-market rates?"

"Darn, right! It's all about spreads, son. Spreads." He smiled and propped his feet up on the table. "Bet you'd like to hear our new slogan now, wouldn't you?"

"Boy, would I!"

Sometimes it pays to sound all Jimmy Olsen during an interview. It reaffirms the interviewer's sense of power. Lets 'em believe they're still in charge. It's called rope-a-dope.

Mike Skull leaned forward, his Southern drawl smooth as jelly. "America's Favorite Bank … when you don't have a choice."

I sat there silent. Not knowing what to say.

"Was it something I said, son? You've got that brain-freeze look on your face."

"Oh no," I said, holding back a roll of my eyes. "I was just pondering the genius behind it all. It's brilliant. Really." (Here comes a beautiful segue.) "And speaking of brilliant, I brought a copy of my past performance reports. I was a consistent top producer in originating home loans at Frontier."

"Don't need it," he said, waving me off. "I already know about your background. Checked on it before I called you. Quite impressive. And only one sick day in your tenure."

"I believe in working hard, sir," I said. "And I think I'd be a great asset to your team."

Big head smiled. "Shoot, I like you, Mr. Foster. If I had a daughter, you'd be the one I'd want diddling her twat. Simple as that. So, I'm through beatin' around the bush. I got to fill this position before Christmas, so I can get on with my merrymaking. You know what I mean?" He leaned forward and squinted. "How does fifty grand a year plus commission sound to you, Hudson? With interest rates in check, and that tiger they call inflation tamed, you should be able to clear around ninety grand next year.

All the bennies included, of course. So what do you say? You my man? You my top gun?"

As heinous as this man might seem to you right now, he was the only person offering me a job. The only man concerned about my dirty underwear (figuratively speaking of course). So, at this moment in my life, I stashed away my crusader's cap by telling myself that life ain't perfect. I ain't perfect. And that sometimes you're going to have to work for people you don't like or respect. Sometimes you don't have a choice. Besides, I told myself, there was nothing illegal going on here. Just good old-fashioned capitalism at its finest. I decided I was going to take this job and love it. And even if I didn't love it, at least it would act as a springboard to bigger and better things. Only one thing still bothered me.

"I have to tell you, Mr. Skull. I haven't even filled out an application yet."

"Formality only," he said.

"But I passed another applicant in the hall."

"The Stanford MBA?"

"I'm not sure."

"The leggy brunette?"

"Yeah. That's the one."

He waved a hand in dismissal. "Forget about her. She's too much of a looker. Half the sales force would be trying to get in her pants, including me." He shook his head. "Nope. Simply can't risk it."

"So then what you're saying," I said, my words full of hope, "is that I've got the job?"

"That's what I'm saying, Hudson." He got up slowly and fetched an application from a nearby credenza. "I mean as long as you're not a druggie, and your background checks don't reveal you just slaughtered a family of four in a Vermont log cabin or something, then yeah, you're my man."

"I'm no criminal," I said. "And I don't do drugs."

"I believe you, son," he said, walking toward me. "It's all just a formality. Something to keep human resources busy." He placed the application in front of me. "You can fill it out here or at home. Whatever's convenient for you. Just make sure you have it back to me by Winsdee at noon. That'll give me ample time to process it. And if everything checks out okay, which I expect it will, then we'll chug a holiday cocktail together." He flashed me a robber-baron smile. "On me."

"Sounds great," I said. "And I'm going to fill out the application right now, so you'll have it back today. Also if you need me to pee in a cup, I'm ready for that too."

"No cups necessary, Hudson. Just a lock of your hair will do." He pulled out a pair of scissors from his back pocket and positioned himself behind me. "I'm no barber, but I'm no butcher either. So hold still." I felt a small tug at the base of my scalp, then heard the snap of scissors.

"I usually charge for samples," I said.

"Most celebrities do," he said. "There, all done. And don't worry. You can't even tell." He showed me my hair sample all tucked away neatly in a little plastic bag.

"That's it?" I asked.

"That's it," he said. "Just leave the application with Sarah, the receptionist, on your way out."

"So when do I start?"

"How 'bout Mundee, the twenty-eighth. My hangover should be gone about then." Another robber-baron smile, only deadlier this time.

I laughed, if only to let him think he was funny. You do that sometimes when 90K is on the line. We both stood up and shook hands violently, like two cattle ranchers who had just closed escrow on the Ponderosa.

"Welcome aboard, Hudson," he said. "Welcome aboard."

-17-

MR. PERFECT HAD WARNED me about credit cards—about how vulnerable I'd be to their siren song. *Hey, buddy? You're not broke. You got $25,000 worth of plastic right in your back pocket. That's right, Mack. Why don't you take me out on the town, and I'll show you a real good time. Just you and me. Whaddaya say?* Up until now I had somewhat heeded my father's advice on the evils of credit, but with my new job and all, I figured it was okay to start "charging" full steam ahead.

I had it all figured out. If I were to start on December 28, then my first paycheck would be on the first of January. (It was a beautiful move on my part. Narrowing the lag time between your start date and your first paycheck is always a smart move. Time is money.) That maneuver would give me a few hundred dollars in my pocket to tide me over until the fifteenth. It would cover incidentals like food (SpaghettiOs and peanut butter), gas, and welcome-aboard lunches with my new colleagues who promised to "spring" for lunch but never did. With incidentals covered, all I had to do was stall my landlord for a few days. Float the check in the mail via Italy and plead ignorance. I had never been late before on the rent, so there would be no reason for them to suspect anything now. As far as my car payment and credit card bills were concerned, I had a fifteen-day grace period on them. *Boom.* A few more timely floats and all would be black again on my balance sheet. I mean who needs financial software when you've got a mind like mine, right?

So there I went. Charging into the Christmas season like a transformed Scrooge. Buying presents for everyone at the drop of a hat. American Express. Visa. MasterCard.

What do you need? I've got it all!

Now, if you want, you can picture me starring in one of those cornball movie montages. You know, where some thin rock song accompanies my shopping spree. There's me trying on expensive suits. Me spinning in front of the mirror and getting a thumbs-up from a jolly tailor. Me trying on shoes. Me flirting with the sales lady and getting a dirty look from her frumpy bald-headed manager. And finally, me crossing Rodeo Drive with eight shopping bags in hand, stopping traffic in a two-thousand-dollar Italian suit.

I gotta tell ya. Chicks were digging me.

Now picture me opening the front door to my apartment, bags in hand, and the cheesy rock song fading out into reality. That's when the phone rings. That's when it always rings. Just like in the movies.

"Hello."

"Hudson Foster?"

"Yes?"

"Mike Skull." I didn't like the sound of his voice. It had that bad-day-at-Black-Rock tone.

"Merry Christmas, Mike," I said, trying to play through the bad karma.

"I wish I could say it was."

"What's wrong?" I asked, panicking. "'Cause I swear to God I didn't inhale. Secondhand smoke, I tell ya! Secondhand smoke!"

"Relax, son. You passed the drug test. That's not it."

"Then what? *What?*"

A long pause, then a clearing of his Southern throat. "Well, if you want to know how the cow ate the cabbage, son, here it is. We found a deuce on your record. What we call a 502, or in layman's terms, a drunk driving. That's a criminal offense in the State of California. You want to tell me about it?"

I must confess to you now. It was true. I made a dumb mistake. I was convicted of drunk driving. But, thank God, nobody got hurt. It all happened on a Friday the thirteenth. I had been partying all night in this underground nightclub in Hollywood—a wild club that looked like a *Star Wars* set. I remember purple stalactites hanging from the ceiling, a Mars-red mist crawling across the dance floor, and a host of model types slinking about the smoke-filled cave in plastic and rubber. I don't remember much else, except for the brightly colored martinis being served. I had my share, though. I do remember that. But the sad thing is—I don't even remember getting in my car.

According to the police, I ran a red light. And when they pulled me over, they said I looked white as a ghost riding on autopilot, like one of those crash test dummies. I vaguely remember being asked to take a piss somewhere foreign, and the next thing I knew, I woke up in a puke-filled jail cell, a bunch of boozehounds just like me writhing on the floor.

So much for the work hard, play hard credo.

We all stirred about the same time the guard opened the cell door, groaning and moaning and looking like death warmed over. Then for some stupid reason, every one of those stiffs picked me to dump on. (I guess I just have that comforting presence.)

There was the rat-faced embezzler from Beverly Hills who tried to go to "sleep" with a bottle of Smirnoff and a batch of 'ludes—

thought he had died and gone to heaven and I was his guardian angel. *Is that you, Clarence?* Then there was the washed-up Hollywood actor who had plowed his run-down Mercedes into the local multiplex. His face was so bloated I couldn't tell where the plastic surgery left off and the accident kicked in. *Normally I don't look this bad in the morning, señor.* And finally, this piggish guy in a soiled UCSB sweat suit who, during a March Madness basketball game (this of course questionable coming from him), gulped down an entire pony keg of Schlitz malt liquor, then hopped in his car to get cigarettes and, for some strange reason, found himself doing donuts on his neighbor's front lawn. *Any word on who won the Valparaiso game?*

I remember feeling humiliated by it all, ashamed, but also very lucky that I had not caused anybody any harm. When Gardner bailed me out (Mr. Perfect was never told), I swore to myself that I'd never drink and drive again. And I haven't. And I won't. Remember? That's why I said I only had one beer at Gardner's that day. And even then, I gave it ample time to burn off. Don't get me wrong, I'm no teetotaler, and I'm not trying to take the fun out of the party. I'm just tryin' to keep us all safe in a fast-paced world. That's all.

I don't care what you do. Just don't get in the car with a heat on. Period.

And if you think I'm playin' with you, check this out. That whole freaky scene went down five years ago. And up until today I thought I had paid for my crime. But now it was coming back to haunt me in other ways. Apparently a drunk driving charge stays on your record for ten years. Ten years! I had no idea that it was something employers checked. Holy blackout, Batman! I was in a pinch. I decided to keep it simple. Play it straight with Mr. Skull.

"I made a mistake," I said. "I went to a nightclub with some friends and had a few beers. Then I got in my car and ran a red light. There were no crashes or burning bodies. I was just over the limit. I made a mistake, Mr. Skull, and I'm really sorry that it happened. And I guarantee you that it will never happen again."

He cleared his throat, then said in an understanding voice, "Hey, I've been in your shoes, Hudson. Had a couple of deuces myself. But that was back in the good old days when drinking was the cool thing to do. Unfortunately, nobody wants to hire Happy-Hour Hudson anymore—can't take a chance on you pulling an Henri Paul at the Christmas party. Unfortunately, management frowns upon nonperforming assets. I'm sorry, Hudson."

"But I made a mistake."

"They're not leaving room for mistakes anymore, son. Not today, I'm afraid. Not unless you're famous, of course, or the president. The truth is it's not enough just to compete in this day and age. You gotta stick the landing."

I lost my temper. "Now you listen here, you cowpokin' pea brain. You promised me! You promised me!"

"You promised me you were no criminal."

He had me there. And no amount of ranting and raving and bullying would change the situation. I did the only other thing I could think of. I begged. Begged for my life. "Please, Mr. Skull. I need this job. There must be something I can do. *Something.* Let me talk to the president."

A ten-second silence, then a whisper. "Hold on a minute." I heard a door close in the background. He got back on the phone. "There is one thing, Hudson. But only because I like you. And I believe you."

"Anything."

"Well, I happen to know this girl who works down at the courthouse." His voice was low now, like a spy's in a phone booth.

"I know her well, if you get my drift. Anyway, for a thousand dollars, I can have your record cleaned up. But the window is small. They're busy transferring the old data into a new computer system—getting prepared for the Y2K bug. And everyone knows information gets lost during these transfers. Files disappear. Life goes on."

"You mean like—"

"Like it never happened."

"There must be some other way," I said. "I'm not comfortable with that ... it's illegal."

"It's just business, Hudson. Just business."

"Not where I come from."

"Where you come from doesn't exist anymore, son. Today, honesty only leaves you hungry."

So there it was. An offer on the table. For a cool grand I could buy my way out of a jam—erase responsibility forever. Who would it hurt, you ask? Well I'll tell you who it would hurt. Me, that's who. And you. I had made that mistake once before in my life. Bought my way out of a jam. Took the easy way out and did something I knew was wrong. I'm not going to get into it now, because it wasn't a life-or-death situation. In fact, only a few people would even know about it. Those being my partners in crime of course. But you know what? I didn't get away with anything. Because I carried the guilt inside for a long time before I finally forgave myself. I felt a lot like Raskolnikov. And believe me, redemption through suffering is no way to go. We all make mistakes that we're not proud of. I know I have. After all, we're only human. The key is in knowing when it's a mistake, recognizing it, and vowing never to repeat it again. It's called character. And you know what? Your character will be tested every day. You'll have the opportunity to buy anything. Final exams.

Licenses. Degrees. People. Anything and everything in the back room. But it's not right, and it never will be. Even though people will tell you that it is. Everybody does it, they'll say. And it's tempting—real tempting—because the hardest thing in this world is taking the legal route out, while your buddies are taking shortcuts and driving fancy cars. They'll tell you that life ain't black or white anymore, that a new gray area has emerged in the business world, and that it's a lot harder to see the line. And I agree with them. It is a lot harder to see the line. But my philosophy on the line is simple. If you're screwing someone else to get ahead, then you've probably crossed that line—whether you can see it or not. And if you knowingly cross that line repeatedly, then I hope you get what's coming to you. And the next time I see your ugly mug, I hope it's a police artist's sketch on the front page.

But if you're one of those good guys who's sitting on the fence in a tight spot, wondering if it's the right thing to do, then believe me it's not. And if you're sittin' there right now, rollin' your eyes and thinking I'm some goody-two-shoes spouting off about something I don't know—then think again. Because I've been there. Seen the dark side. Seen people cheat life and watched the fiber of their characters rot with every lie and scam. And believe me, it ain't pretty. It breaks people every day.

Needless to say, I thanked Mr. Skull for the opportunity. I was broke. But I wasn't broken.

"Good luck, Mr. Foster."

-18-

CONGRATULATIONS. YOU MADE it to the last chapter. And before we go to Mr. Perfect's Christmas party, I want to take this opportunity to personally thank you for hanging out with me this long—for giving an old bag-o'-wind like me your time in a hectic world. I know you're all anxious to find out who that dude is wearing the TINSTAAFL hat in my dreams. I know I am. So take my hand and I'll give you a Peter Pan ride back in time. But stay close. I hear there's asteroids out there.

Picture us flying through space now, spiraling down toward planet Earth. It is Christmas Eve in Los Angeles, close to the turn of the century, and last-minute shoppers scurry about the malls on a starry night. And if you look real close, out toward the dark Pacific Ocean, you can see a guy on a beach cruiser bicycle pedaling furiously down a crowded street. No, over there. The guy with the orange reflectors on his shoes. He is wearing a long black coat that is flapping in the breeze, steering with one hand and clutching a nicely gift-wrapped present in the other. That'd be me, on my way to Mr. Perfect's house. We're in Marina del Rey now, a tiny seaside community just south of Venice Beach. This is where my father lives—in a high-rise condominium that overlooks all of L.A. He's not rich. But he's done pretty darn well for himself. And, by the way, since this is kind of a long chapter, I'm going to do you a favor and break it down into two acts and one intermission. That's just the kind of guy I am. So get yourself comfortable under the old oak tree and read on. You'll be glad you did.

ACT 1

Broke, befuddled, esteem running at dangerously low levels, I arrived at my father's front door on Christmas Eve at exactly 5:45 p.m. Still no sign of Santa. And just to give you an idea on how low I was feeling at the time, I'm going to share my stats with you. Looking back on it, they wouldn't even have accepted me as a contestant on one of those lousy singles game shows. So if you would, picture my sad face frozen on screen in a state of shock as the sound of a typewriter zips these words across my image.

Hudson Foster: single

Occupation: unemployed

Prospects: none that he can think of.

Assets: nineteen dollars in a checking account. Two bucks in pocket. (Not counting the "lucky penny" he just found in the elevator.)

Liabilities: car loan $23,000

Credit cards: $15,000

Net worth: ($37,979)

Situation: desperate

Short-term goals: borrow jing from Dad.

Laying yourself out on paper can really wake you up—something you should only try at home. I figured if I had to, I could sell my car and trade down. I had a little equity left in the

Bimmer and my credit was still good. But it was the fifteen grand in credit cards that would haunt me for years to come. It was then that I realized I was still paying off a Visa card from the nineteen eighties. I figured at the rate I was going—making minimum payments—it would take me until I was sixty-three years old to pay them off! Friggin' credit cards. They make it seem so darn easy to spend, don't they? But let me tell you one thing, the minute you miss a payment on those cards, they send in the attack dogs. And I'm not gonna go all Charles Dickens on you right now, but trust me, the minute the collection department puts you on automatic dialer, your life becomes instant hell. Some hardballer named Lou gets paid eight bucks an hour just to grind the crap out of you and wear you down. You pay either way. And it's a bad scene, man. It really is. Quite the opposite from when they first contacted you.

Congratulations, Mr. Foster, you have achieved a level in life that most people only dream about. It's always the same sales pitch that gets you. Whether you get a call from a young college girl with a Bambi-soft voice reading haltingly from a canned script, a letter in the mail, or are suckered into signing up at a school booth, they all play on your sense of self-worth, telling you what a big success you are even if you don't have a dime to your name. And it makes you feel good, important, like you're J. Paul Getty and just need a bridge loan until the banks open in the morning. Well, I'll let you in on a little secret. If you don't have any dough, then a borrowed dollar is not your friend. Because you've got to pay it back. And believe me, paying back credit card debt is no picnic. And the farther in debt you get, the more likely you are to be working for the "man" for the rest of your life. And who wants that? So give yourself a chance—pay cash—and you'll be truly free to pursue your dreams.

And now, back to our regularly scheduled story ...

Standing at the door that night with my hand on the knob, I remember thinking about how pathetic my life had become—about how I had let my father and myself down for not having "made it" in this material world. It is a familiar trap we all fall into with our parents, I think. Because all of us want to grow up better than they did—want to live for the day when we can pick up the check at the restaurant or plunk down fifty grand on an overpriced Miami condo just so they can retire in style and comfort by the beach. It's our own little way of thanking them for raising such a success. But when our plans don't turn out the way we expect them to, then we start blaming ourselves. I know I did. It used to be that I wrote out all these stupid goals in a nice and neat little notebook—scheduled my life down to a tee. Stuff like where do I see myself in five years, ten years, twenty years from now? *Become a millionaire by age twenty-one. Make partner by age twenty-eight. Buy a home free and clear in Brentwood by thirty-two.* But it wasn't until I lost a job that I realized that these were all money goals. All goals designed to feed my own selfish existence. The worst part was when I didn't come close to achieving them, I got all pissed off at myself and, consequently, the world around me. I started aiming for little old ladies in the crosswalk and snapping at strangers for looking at me wrong. All because I didn't accomplish my goals that year. I don't think like that anymore. I found out I didn't need stuff—I needed people. So anytime anybody ever asks me where I'll be in the next twenty years, I always answer with the same pat response, "Hopefully with family and friends." I guess you could say I've broadened my horizons. Upsized my thoughts.

At any rate, I thought I'd share that with you, because it took me a long time to get to the point of letting go. But unfortunately, on that one certain Christmas Eve, I was still my own worst enemy, and I needed something or someone to show me the way. I didn't know it at the time, but what waited for me inside that night was not money, not a movie ending where the townspeople show up with a basket of cash to bail me out, but something much more special. Something that I'd possessed all along but was too blinded by ambition to see. And no, it wasn't a pair of ruby-red slippers if that's what you're thinking … it was my family.

When I finally opened the door that night and walked in, colored streamers fell from the ceiling, plump balloons swirled around the room, and a raucous chorus of "Merry Christmas, Hudson!" rang out from the crowd. Suddenly I was having my hand pumped by Mr. Perfect in the entrance hall (Italian marble for those wondering), and several people were patting me on the back. I remember, at the time, I had mixed feelings about this reception. I didn't know if I felt more like the one millionth shopper at a grocery store or a war hero returning home with a Purple Heart and two hooks for hands.

"Merry Christmas, son," said my father, hugging me.

"Merry Christmas, Dad," I said, trying hard to get into the spirit of the season. I held up his present. (A boxed CD set of Sinatra.) "I brought you a little something."

My father smiled. "Thank you, son," he said. "That'll look real fine under the tree. Real fine."

"Dad, I didn't have a lobotomy," I said. "I'm just out of a job."

He laughed nervously, placed his hands on my shoulders, and spun me around toward the living room crowd. He said, "All right, people, listen up. This here's my boy, Hudson. Due to the recent mega-mergers in the financial services industry, he finds himself temporarily outsourced. For those of you looking for an exceptional employee, this might be your lucky day—your only chance to grab a superstar. He's bright, a hard worker, and would be a major asset to any company."

"Yeah, but can he dance?" someone yelled from the crowd. Laughter followed.

"Not as good as his old man," my father answered. "By the way, offers start at forty thousand a year plus commission—and all the bennies he can eat. So talk with him. Mingle. And have fun." He raised a finger into the air. "And remember to use coasters."

Great, I thought. My father had turned Christmas Eve into a job fair. At this point all I wanted to do was see my sister and get the heck out of there. Say good-bye and hop a rail into Palmdale. Maybe hole up in some cheap motel room and wait out the apocalypse.

"Dad, is Hill here yet?" I asked.

"She'll be here in a little while," he said. "She's at her boyfriend's parents' house." He nudged me forward. "Now get out there and mingle. There's some big hitters out there waiting to talk with you."

"Hey, John," another yelled from the crowded room, "can we get some tunes on in here?"

"Coming right up," said my father, heading for the entertainment center, eager to plow through his CD collection.

When it came to raising a family, my father was all business. But to his friends he was the life of the party. I could only guess as to what might blast through the surround-sound speakers. Neil Diamond was the odds-on favorite, but Celine Dion was running a very close second. (A blatant crush on the "sultry diva" had punished us all for well over a year.) But I wasn't gonna count out Garth Brooks either. One of Mr. Perfect's New Year's resolutions was to embrace more "new music."

I watched as my father strutted out into the holiday crowd with his head held high, his square jaw jutting, his back ramrod straight—not one inch of his powerful being out of place.

As usual, his military-cut salt-and-pepper hair ... *was perfect.*

He was clad in his favorite uniform on this evening of joy: blue blazer, green slacks, black loafers, and a white open-collared shirt.

Come to think of it, that's what I was wearing.

"Nice place your dad's got here," came a nasally voice. I turned in the candle-lit entrance hall and spotted two men dressed in black undertaker suits staring at me funny. I returned the favor, sizing them up. They were garden-hose thin, fortyish, with reptilian faces and greasy coal hair parted in the middle. Both had pasty white skin and mutton-chop sideburns—sly smiles as thin as dimes.

"Yeah, he's proud of it," I said, looking away, staring into the splendor that was Mr. Perfect's designer three-bedroom condo. About fifty people were enjoying its festive ambiance, I noticed, most of them getting jacked on Napa Valley red and grocery store eggnog.

The basic color scheme of my father's bachelor pad—black furniture and high-fashion gray carpet—had been chosen by an ex-girlfriend in the late eighties. Mr. Perfect had already been through the distressed look, as well as the early American stage, and felt no need to change for change's sake now. The huge living room—which housed a modest Christmas tree and several bulbous decorations—was made up of black leather couches, glass coffee tables, and colorful Picasso prints. (Most of which had been obtained at a considerable discount with the help of another ex-girlfriend who worked in the print department of the Butterfield and Butterfield auction house in Beverly Hills. It was a short-lived relationship that had apparently ended over an argument about Mormon missionaries "saving souls" in Papua New Guinea. She for. He against.) The back corner of the living room consisted of a wet bar, a big-screen TV, and a table of hors d'oeuvres. All of which were framed nicely by floor-to-ceiling windows that overlooked the vast Pacific Ocean and the twinkling city lights below. *"Like scattered jewels across a black carpet,"* as Mr. Perfect was fond of saying.

"I'm Frank Jardeen," said one of the men dressed in black, finally breaking our uncomfortable silence. "This here's my brother Larry."

"Nice to meet you," I said, shaking hands with both of them in two quick pumps. I was hoping for a fast getaway. But alas, across the room, I could see my father clenching his jaw at me, monitoring the situation over by the Christmas tree. It was—I had come to know—his famous proactive nod.

Frank Jardeen said, "It sure is a tragedy about the financial disorder. I mean about all the layoffs and mergers."

I flashed him a pre-eggnog smile just as Neil Diamond's "Cracklin' Rosie" piped over the sound system.

"Global chaos," I said. "What are you gonna do?"

He shook his head. "I guess it couldn't be helped."

"Nope," I said, glancing down at my shoes. "I guess it couldn't."

Larry, the other brother, and the more serious and dour looking of the two, chimed in with his deep voice. "Let me ask you a question, Hudson."

"Shoot," I said.

"Did you like your job? Did it bring your soul personal satisfaction and fulfillment? Or was it merely a means to a paycheck?"

That was three questions. But to call him on that now meant longer conversation and thus the delay of the downing of my first cocktail.

"I didn't hate it," I said.

"That bad, huh?" Larry scratched his long mutton-chop sideburn, then gave his brother that back-to-you-Bob look.

"You see, Hudson," said Frank Jardeen, taking over, "all across America, people are reaching out for something much more spiritual. The new millennium is literally changing the way we feel about ourselves."

I'll tell you what I was really getting tired of hearing about. The new millennium. Millennium this. Millennium that. Millennium smack. Just another marketing crock is what I thought about it.

"Yeah," I said, hoping to freak these guys out. "I feel a real change in the air myself. It's called Armageddon."

To my dismay, my negative front was greeted with glee. "That would be *wonderful*," said Frank Jardeen. "And do you know why it would be wonderful, Hudson?"

"Because Dr. Kevorkian would be out of a job?"

"Yes," he answered, not missing a beat. "But it also means our business would boom." He fiddled a moment with an old-time pocket watch, glanced at his pale-faced brother, and then looked me straight in the eye with his grinning skull-like face. "How would you like to be involved in a real growth industry with no down cycles? An industry with fresh air and green trees?"

"I thought the Marlboro Man job was already taken."

"You're funny," said the Jardeen brothers in unison, no smiles in sight. "We like funny."

After a deep moment of thought, Larry Jardeen hit me with his deep baritone. "We're in the *preneed* business, Hudson. Helping people move on into the afterlife with ease and comfort. That's what we do."

"As in the Grim Reaper?"

Frank Jardeen glanced at his brother, then turned a crooked smile my way. "Death is indeed our business, but if you can get by the macabre and get to the numbers, then you just might find a very solid and lucrative future awaits you in the exciting field of expiration. Six figures is the norm." He pulled out a black business card from his jacket pocket and handed it to me. Their official titles were funeral directors. How uplifting, I thought. Should I start high-kicking like a Rockette now, or later?

"We run the To-Die-For Brothers Mortuary Corporation, Hudson. Twenty-four outlets nationwide and growing. That means many opportunities in memorial property purchase sales, embalming, and, not to mention, body removal."

Oh, goody.

"Frankly, Hudson," said the deep-voiced Larry. "We're bullish on bereavement."

I felt my stomach turn. I don't do death very well. That's why I couldn't follow in my father's insurance footsteps. Talking about death benefits all day made me queasy. I mean part of finding the right job is knowing what you're good at. But just as important is knowing what you're not good at. And anyway you sliced it, the Jardeen brothers were dealing with dead bodies on a daily basis. And I couldn't go there.

"I appreciate the offer guys, but—"

Frank Jardeen stopped me in mid-getaway by placing a large skeletal hand on my shoulder. His face had the pale, bluish glow of a cadaver. "It's only natural to feel this way, Hudson. Most people react a little funny at first. But you'll get used to it—trust me. And with the baby boomers dying off in record numbers, your financial future will be secure well into the next century. All signs point to growth. And let's be honest. What business today but ours actually welcomes Armageddon?"

I don't know why, but that movie *Soylent Green* came to mind. Conveyor belts and crackers. I suddenly felt sick, and I knew I had to bolt before I blew chow right there on Larry's pointy black funeral director shoes.

"I'll think about it," I said, edging away from them, still clutching my father's gift. "We'll do lunch. Talk embalming. I promise."

As I pushed my way through the holiday crowd, the Jardeen brothers shouted in unison, "1-800-caskets!"

Seconds later I ducked frantically into the kitchen, hoping for a little privacy. No such luck. I didn't even have a chance to catch my breath.

"Is that Hudson Foster?"

I turned my head and saw Ralph "Backfat" Swerdlow with his thick red buffalo face peeking out of my father's Sub-Zero refrigerator—a three-martini grin plastered on his jowly mug. (Warning: meeting this guy may cause side effects. If nausea, vomiting, or headaches occur, please consult your doctor.)

"How ya doin', Ralph?" I said reluctantly. I looked around the corner to make sure the formaldehyde brothers weren't stalking me.

"Tits," answered Backfat, lifting a bottle of Chardonnay from the refrigerator and placing it down on the center island. "Just tits."

The word *tits* coming from a sixty-year-old fat man ought to give you some idea about the sincerity of this individual. He was my father's stockbroker and lived across the hall. Although he had been in Los Angeles for the better part of thirty years, he still carried a thick Brooklyn accent that made him sound like a mobster.

We called him "Backfat" because of the obvious—the excessive rolls of tired flesh that hung down from his neck and back like deflated tires. And speaking of tits. He had quite a pair himself— double Ds, in fact. Trust me. You don't want to glimpse this guy at the pool.

He was housed tonight in a stained yellow polo shirt (which was as big as a tent), white tennis shorts, and aqua-blue deck shoes. As usual, his curly pubic-red hair glistened with gel, matching the sparkle of two gold chains that hung down from his monster neck. No doubt souvenirs left over from an eight-year bull market.

"What's eatin' you, Hudson?" asked the perfect cover boy for *Glutton* magazine. "You look a little spooked."

"Just a little tired is all."

He laughed while corking the wine. "All that holiday job hunting got you down, huh? How 'bout a drink?"

"Love one," I said.

He poured me a brimmer in a bubble glass. I didn't wait for him to pick it up and hand it to me. I just grabbed it off the counter and chug-a-lugged shamelessly. Backfat looked surprised.

"A little down on your luck, are ya, pal?"

"Whatever gave you that idea?" I burped a few letters of the alphabet, then changed the subject quickly. "How's Ralphie?"

"Fine," said Backfat. "He's making five hundred grand a year."

Ralphie was his lunkhead son. And anytime you ever asked Backfat how his son was doing, he was always "making five hundred grand a year." Not that I doubted it. Not when you've got a daddy who owned half of California. Backfat, despite his slovenly appearance, was worth well over two hundred million dollars. Earlier in the year, his fat mug had graced the covers of every financial magazine in the country. *Money. Worth. Businessweek.* And *Fortune*—where he wore a cowboy hat and a stupid grin with a bold caption tucked under his three chins: *"Why is this money manager cashing out of the market?"*

Backfat was no dummy. Greedy as heck. But no dummy. He cashed out before the summer crash and was now doing what all rich people do after making that much money. Ballooning over the Arctic. Riding Harleys in the wine country. And the latest, building a boat from scratch and retracing the Vikings' route into some strange but not quite so new land.

"Is your high-rolling son showing up tonight?" I asked. "Gonna grace us with his charming presence?" (Charming presence translated: rude, ugly, pimple-faced doofus who lights his farts.)

"Don't think so," said Backfat, nibbling on a chunk of Gouda. "He's trolling for chicks down at the Rainbow."

"The rock club on Sunset?"

"Yeah, he knows the bartender. Says the easiest time to score pussy is on Christmas Eve. Easy pickin's to comfort a groupie away from her family." He chuckled, then took a swig of wine. "Tell me something, Hudson. How is it a guy can be out of work in a market with the unemployment rate the lowest it's been in twenty-eight years?"

I leaned against the center island. "They call it banking," I said, blowing out a disgusted sigh. "Banking."

Backfat smiled. "I told you some years ago, Hudson. Bankers don't make squat. Never an upside in banking. You've got to start your own business today, if you expect any kind of take-home pay at all. What with the tax system the way it is."

"Then how does one accumulate wealth with Uncle Sam?"

Backfat peeked inside the fridge, shuffled a few condiments around, and pulled out some mustard. "Simple," he said, looking up and smiling. "You cheat."

"Tell me something I don't know," I said, disgusted.

"Look, Hudson," he said. "Let me give you a little bit of the old Swerdlow savvy. You got to get aggressive out there. Years ago I found myself in your shoes—out of a job in a boom market. Then I answered a classified ad. It said to ask for a Mr. Chase. Now automatically right there you know you're dealing with a guy from the old school, right? The ad says 'closers only.' So I call up. Two ringee-dingees later, some hard guy answers.

"*Yeah?*'

"'Is Mr. Chase in?' I ask.

"*Name?*' the voice says harshly.

"'The name's Swerdlow. You Mr. Chase?'

"*Maybe.*'

"'Maybe,' I says. Almost ready to pull the guy through the wire and wring his sorry neck. He's playing with me now. Testing my mettle. And I know it's him. So I give it right back.

"'Are you or aren't you?' I demand.

"The guy answers in his New York voice.

"*Are you a closa?*'

"'Course I'm a closer,' I say.

" '*Yeah. I'm Mr. Chase,*' the slimeball finally says. Like he doesn't give a shit. Then he says, '*How can I help ya?*'

"'Looking for a job, sir.'

" '*You are, are ya? Ever sold any big-ticket items over the phone befo? Oil? Gas? Computas?*'

"This is where I got gnarly, Hudson, and decided to grab the interview by the fucking balls and squeeze." (I promised you I wouldn't cuss anymore. But I can't control the others.)

"'Listen here, Mr. Chase,' I says. 'Cut the crap. You want to give me a fucking interview, or do I come through this fucking wire and rip your heart out?'

"Mr. Chase didn't hesitate, Hudson. He says to me, '*Get your fuckin' ass o-va here, you sorry piece of crap. You passed the interview. You got the job.*"

Backfat leaned his lumpy ass against the refrigerator door and crossed his fleshy arms. "True story."

INTERMISSION

I think we all need a little break after Ralph "Backfat" Swerdlow. So go ahead and take this opportunity to hit the head, feed the cat, or whatever it is you've gotta do. Then we'll head for the homestretch, seek out that guy in the TINSTAAFL hat, and call it a day. I know I promised you a short story.

ACT 2

Meanwhile, back at the ranch, Backfat and I were still hiding out in Mr. Perfect's stainless-steel kitchen—not a crumb out of place. Backfat was sitting on the center island, smoking a Cuban cigar, his short, pink, fire-hydrant legs crossed like a girl. I was busy pouring my third goblet of Chardonnay. I knew I couldn't hang out in there forever, but I was going to try. Eventually Mr. Perfect would seek me out and push me into the fray. It was only a matter of time.

And so, at this very moment, I felt like a nervous comedian waiting backstage, knowing full well that his time in the spotlight was near.

"Shouldn't you be out there pressing the flesh?" asked Backfat, a crumpled smoke ring falling from his greasy lips. "I mean, a job ain't going to jump up and bite you in the ass."

"If you're so concerned about my welfare, Ralph, then why don't you invest two million in a little Internet start-up company I've got going? How 'bout it? You in?"

"Sorry, fresh out," he said. "But you're on the right track."

That was what I liked most about Backfat. His ability to kick a man while he was down—and like it. I never had an Internet company. But I thought I'd show you how tough it is to raise seed money for any venture. By being overly aggressive and straight to the point, you can usually flush out anybody who might be willing to help you along the way. I could forget about Backfat. He was a taker par excellence. Don't get me wrong. I don't object to anybody making a lot of dough. I just hate to see people who don't give something back.

"I mean, I'd ask you to join my firm," said Backfat, talking with his mouth full, "but I don't think you got what it takes. Sellin' stocks is a hard sell."

"I'm not interested in selling stocks for your firm," I said. "I mean, any financial company that doesn't eat its own cooking is suspect in my book."

Backfat licked his lips and grinned.

"You sound like a man outta dough, Hudson. Are you … *outta dough?*"

It is these kinds of sarcastic remarks that usually propel you for better or worse (mostly worse) to want to keep up with the Joneses. I was tempted to go with the passionate I'll-show-you speech, but, proud to say, I was past that now. As we learned earlier, this type of response is just a defensive maneuver to mask jealousy for the want of material goods.

"That's none of your business, Swerdlow," I said, looking away. "Besides, what's it to you?"

"You talk real confident for a poor man, Hudson. Probably think your daddy's gonna bail you out. Well think again, maestro. I know your pa's net worth. Trust me, you're on your own."

More positive advice from a grown-up.

"And what about your son?" I said. "Talk about nepotism. You set him up at your firm with a one-million-dollar trading account. I mean, it doesn't take a genius to make money in a bull market, Backfat. And I know, because I went to high school with your son. He's an idiot—a real live buffoon. I mean, anybody that admits to beating off to the soundtrack of *Platoon* and liking it is screwed up in my book. Face it. Your son has nothing to offer society."

"And you do?"

"You bet I do, fat boy. And it's pointing out parasites like you."

"Noble words from such a young man. You must be an old soul—

or the last of the white hats." He laughed and scratched his belly. "You know, I can just look at a guy and tell you how much money he makes. It's in the way he carries himself. The way he walks and talks. The way he blames others for having what he doesn't have."

"I may not have a lot of money, *Nerdlow,* but I've got my dignity. And I've got a good sense of right and wrong. And I'm not going to sacrifice moral accountability just for dough. That's the difference between me and you."

"Money creates its own morality, Hudson. Simple as that. Your problem is you believe in God."

I have always believed in God. Even if I didn't go to church every Sunday. My philosophy on being the best human being I could be meant believing that I would live forever.

"You think I envy you, Swerdlow?" I said. "You think I live to buy people and pleasure?"

Backfat grabbed his crotch and smiled.

"Success matters only as long as you can get it up," he said. "I mean, what else is there in this world but pleasure? You eat, drink, and fuck. What can I tell you, Hudson? Life ain't fair."

I remember asking myself back then, if Lardo here had a coronary in my presence, would I perform the obligatory CPR? The answer was a resounding NO. Pop goes the weasel.

Life ain't fair, but it does have a peculiar way of evening out sometimes.

"Hudson! Hudson!"

It was Mr. Perfect. He stormed into the kitchen like a cop entering a crack house. "There you are," he said. "People have been looking for you." He smoothed down his blazer and shot Backfat a look.

"Me and your son here were just talking business," said Backfat. "Told him I had a couple of real good stock tips for him. Too bad he's out of money."

"He's not out of money, Ralph," my father said. "He's just temporarily out of a job."

Backfat eased his gooey body off the center island, smashed out his cigar in a crystal ashtray, then waddled toward the door. "Well, it's been fun, guys. It really has. But I gotta run. My massage awaits. Happy endings for all." He smiled obscenely. "Merry Christmas, Hudson. And good luck on that job hunt."

"See you at the next stock market crash," I said, shaking my fists at him. "I'll be looking for the biggest tub of goo falling forty stories."

"Hudson!" Mr. Perfect said.

"I can't help it, Dad. That guy just burns me up."

"Well forget about it," he said, "and get in there and start talking with these people."

I was about to grab Mr. Perfect's gift off the counter, but he said, "Forget it." Then he grabbed my shoulders and pushed me toward the door and led me out into the party.

It was time to mix.

Just as we became visible to the festive living room crowd, the soundtrack music from the movie *Titanic* thundered dramatically from the ceiling speakers ... "My Heart Will Go On."

Another Mr. Perfect selection.

People started clapping as we strutted into the shoulder-to-shoulder crowd, the music heralding our arrival, a father and son team walking tall in blue blazers and phony chamber of commerce smiles. I heard someone shout over the din, "Hey, Hudson! Let's hear it for all the tiny Davids who gotta slay Goliath every day!"

Whatever the frick that meant.

Patsy Grubel was the first to pounce on us—a tall, gangly, well-coifed brunette in her late forties, wearing lots of diamonds and a bright green business suit. If it wasn't for a hooknose and the fact that she smelled like a dead bird, you might call her attractive. She used to work with my father, but now she was some type of motivational coach for business executives. I'm not positive, but I think my father nailed her at last year's Christmas party. I saw them both coming out of the bathroom and later saw old Backfat give him an arm nudge and a smile. *"Oh, the wonders of Viagra, huh, Foster?"*

"Hello, John," Patsy said, smiling graciously and holding out a bejeweled hand to be kissed.

"Always a pleasure," said Mr. Perfect. He took her veiny paw and smooched it, much to my dismay. "Hudson, you remember Patsy."

"Yeah," I said, casually looking away. "The seminar lady, right?"

Mr. Perfect smiled apologetically at Patsy for my indifferent tone. Then he turned back to me and whispered out of the corner of his mouth, "She has openings for seminar sales people, son. Be nice."

Patsy chuckled. "It's okay, John. His lax attitude is quite normal after a job loss. He just needs some positive reinforcement, that's all. A little subconscious reprogramming."

Positive reinforcement? Reeducation? Reprogramming? All methods, I'm quite sure, favored by Pol Pot.

"I'm not going to any camps," I said, actively scanning the room for my sister or the guy in the TINSTAAFL hat. But no such luck. All I could see was half the crowd standing around the big-screen TV watching *Rudolph the Red-Nosed Reindeer.* (Mr. Perfect was fond of the classics.)

It was at the end of the program, when Yukon Cornelius brings in the beast and the big white creature deftly places the ornament on the tippy-top of the Christmas tree. Everyone in the room started cheering and clapping at the big finish, each, I'm sure, privately savoring some nostalgic moment when life was simple and they were young.

"I'll leave you two alone for a moment," my father said, smiling sheepishly at Patsy as he backed into the holiday crowd. "I'd better put on a new video ... any requests?"

"How about *It's a Wonderful Life?*" said Patsy. "It's such a positive, upbeat story."

As much as I tried to escape the Jimmy Stewart movie that Christmas, I couldn't. First Gardner had tried to ram it down my throat, now my father.

"Coming right up," said Mr. Perfect.

"Dad, change the music too," I said. "Anything but Madonna—and please, no Paul Anka." Mr. Perfect nodded and shouldered his way through the well-lubed crowd.

I know what you're thinking. You're thinking how can you watch a movie while the music is playing? Simple. You turn down the sound on the TV—and presto! A homemade video. That's the way my father liked it. And after several years of client Christmas parties, his guests had come to love and expect his quirky mix of music and movies. *Rudolph* and the score of *Titanic* had gone over well, but one could only guess as to what might accompany *It's a Wonderful Life.* Last year it had been Billy Idol's "Eyes Without a Face." A marginal hit at best.

Patsy stared at my father's khakied butt as he bent down searching for the video, then turned her Dale Carnegie smile on me. "So, Hudson, tell me about yourself."

"Well, let's see now," I said, looking up and noticing a thistle of mistletoe hanging precariously above our heads. "I like chocolate martinis, cold pizza, women's feet, and sex in the morning. And if that ain't enough, my favorite movie?" A psychotic grin slunk across my face. *"Full … Metal … Jacket."*

She looked at me like I was a T. rex ready to pounce, her thin birdlike lips scrunched into a very serious O. I didn't mean to wipe the Dale Carnegie off her face. But *Tell me about yourself?* Come on. I've always figured that if people couldn't find out about another person through normal human interaction, then they didn't deserve to know. But I'd better warn you. This is the classic "open-ended" question people with "vision" like to ask you. And I don't care if you're flying a spaceship to work in the near future, or interviewing with a bald alien across the desk, you're still going to have to field this banal query at some point in your life. And when that time comes, my advice to you is to keep your response short and sweet.

Patsy crossed her arms like the lady executive she was and said, "I think it's time for a Grubel moment. Don't you agree? Time to say *bye-bye* to the passive-aggressive negativity."

"The what?"

"First, take a deep breath," she said. "And be sure to bring it all the way up from the belly to the throat." This she made clear by demonstrating with her hands. "C'mon, Hudson. Follow me." We both inhaled together, and our stomachs blossomed. "Do you feel the energy bursting through your veins?" she asked.

"Like tiny rocket ships," I said.

"Good. Now exhale." We both blew out our breath at the same time. "Now that our minds are clear," she said, "we're ready for the Grubel mantra."

I watched her set a firm stance, her green business suit hiked up over her bent knees, her red high-heel shoes digging hard into the oyster-gray carpet—her stork-like arms outstretched for balance.

I didn't know if she was going to tackle me or grunt one out.

"Now repeat after me," she said. "On the count of three. And say it like you believe it. Because if you believe it, it will come true."

"Is this some sort of visualization technique?" I said. "Because—"

"Quiet!" she said.

She had caffeine eyes now, like she had just climbed down from Mount Sinai. "Ready," she said, her finger wagging with each count. "One ... two ... three. Life is good! Business is great! People are wonderful! Repeat after me, Hudson!"

She pumped her fists with each screaming affirmation.

"LIFE IS GOOD! BUSINESS IS GREAT! PEOPLE ARE WONDERFUL! AGAIN! LIFE IS GOOD! BUSINESS IS GREAT! PEOPLE ARE WONDERFUL! AGAIN!"

I gave her the small satisfaction of mouthing the words, if only because I felt a slight connection between us due to the simple reason that my father's privates had touched her privates. (Bumping uglies tends to move people closer.) After we had repeated the Grubel mantra a couple more times, she said (still wild-eyed), "Feel free to add to the mantra, Hudson. To custom-fit it to your daily schedule. And like always," she said, slightly out of breath, "I'd love to hear your thoughts and suggestions on my cleansing method."

I was just about to suggest a full-head CAT scan, when a teenage girl shouted, "Look, everybody! Hudson looks just like a young Jimmy Stewart."

I turned my head and saw a mousy blonde in a red snowflake sweater and a white neck brace pointing at the big-screen TV. We all looked. On screen, George Bailey was running frantically through a dark snowy night with desperate eyes and a trickle of blood oozing from the corner of his mouth. Then came Mr. Perfect's music selection—a haunting tune by Roy Orbison aptly titled "Running Scared." It was a surreal video moment, almost Daliesque, and at that instant the room seemed to close in around me—melting, distorting, breathing in and out like a transparent balloon.

Everything became dreamlike and 'shroomy, and all I could see were talking heads jawing at me in slow motion. I still don't recall if I properly excused myself from Patsy Grubel's presence that night. (Not that it really matters. I'm sure a single "cleansing" had purged her tiny brain of any lingering thoughts of my perceived impoliteness.)

All I remember is that I got swept up into a sea of people, getting pinballed from one person to another. It was like I was the point man in the mosh pit at a punk rock concert. Hands were all over me—vying for my attention—touching me like zombies.

Voices came from all sides—all angles.

"Elder law, Hudson. Family Feud. *Now that's the future."*

"Keep your chin up, boy. Get an MBA. You can do it."

"I've got three words for you, Mr. Foster. Internet, broadcast, technology."

"Ostrich farms, pardner. Low in fat. High in protein. Californians will eat it up."

"Two words for ya, palie … ginkgo biloba."

People were breathing all over me, and I couldn't help but inhale the sickening party smells of digested shrimp, cheese balls, Poligrip, and cashew nuts. I spun around to deflect the next talking head, but instead found myself face-to-face with a red furry creature, the "in" Christmas toy of the season. Raucous laughter exploded from its furry mouth, a laugh so maddeningly vile that I wanted to choke it out right there. HA HA HA HA … HA HA HA HA … HA HA HA HA …

My head was spinning, the room was spinning, Roy Orbison was hitting high notes, and all I knew was I had to get the frock out of there—and pronto.

I pushed my way through the shoulder-to-shoulder crowd, the hideous laughter still coming through in waves, brushed by the Christmas tree (knocking off a few ornaments), and dived into Mr. Perfect's office. I slammed the door quickly and closed out the world. It was dark and cool inside, and I didn't bother turning on the lights. All I wanted was a moment to myself, a second to catch my breath and untangle my thoughts.

I leaned back against the smooth wood door, wiped the sweat off my brow, and closed my eyes. The peace and quiet didn't last long.

"Your father throws a pretty mean shindig, don't he, Hudson?"

The voice was soft and understanding, and its grandfatherly tone seemed at home in the dark. Startled, but surprisingly not afraid, I flicked on the light and saw him sitting at my father's computer desk. He was wearing a Santa suit and the TINSTAAFL hat.

"Care to track Old St. Nick's path?" he said. "He should be somewhere over India by now." He booted up the computer, and a blue aquarium glow danced across his rosy cheeks. It was the same guy I had seen in my dreams, and there he was sitting in my father's office working the keyboard. His long white beard was obviously fake, but his thick, bristly gray walrus mustache was authentic. For a minute, I made sure that the scene was real, that I really was in my father's office and not having another dream.

I took mental inventory of the small room just to be sure: black filing cabinets, Mr. Perfect's golf trophy case, the computer workstation, and the same framed black-and-white photographs of my father and me flanking Nolan Ryan at Angel Stadium. It was all too familiar. But I still wasn't convinced that I had actually entered reality. I knew this room too well. And I knew that the only real acid test would be to check the dates on Mr. Perfect's daily "to do" lists.

He made three a day. One for work. One for personal chores. And one for wishes. I walked slowly over to the desk, eyeballed the old geezer, then looked down. As usual, not a pen, pencil, or notepad was out of place. But there were no lists. Usually they were all lined up side by side, each yellow pad with its own silver Cross pen on top. But not tonight. I was convinced I was still asleep. That it would be only a matter of time before I woke up and found myself in bed, my forehead beaded with sweat.

"You looking for these?" The old man opened the desk drawer and pulled out three yellow pads. Then he fanned them out across the wood-grain desk. "I just needed some extra working room to maneuver the mouse—that's all." He smiled warmly, then turned his attention back to the computer. Santa's sleigh, as indicated by a white dot on the screen, was currently servicing Calcutta.

I looked down and picked up the first list. The date at the top of the page read December 24. It was in my father's handwriting— blue ink cursive. It was his personal list, and I noticed that all of the entries had been scratched off. Things like get the car washed, pick up the dry cleaning, call the caterer, etc. It had been another successful day for my father. I glanced down at the next list, his business list, and saw the same date—the same completed results.

But that wasn't what made my heart jump. It was the entry on his wish list that did that. I picked up the third yellow pad, brought it closer to my face, and eyeballed the lone entry. The blue-ink sentence stuck out like a sore thumb across the vast yellow background.

"I wish my son and I would talk more."

It wasn't scratched off.

"I wish I had a father to kick my butt once in a while," said the old man. "Throw me a party when the going got rough."

I looked up and saw him staring at me, his big white eyebrows twitching like caterpillars.

"Who are you?"

"Nobody special." He smiled and crinkles formed around his dull green eyes. "Just a friend of your dad's."

Certainly this was not the response that I wanted to hear. Since I had already accepted this man as some sort of guardian angel, prophet, or keeper of my dreams, I had hoped that he would've made the first move—acknowledged his presence in my sleep. But he didn't. It was then I realized I would have to be the one to flush things out.

"You're looking at me funny, Hudson," he said.

I cleared my throat and set the yellow pad down on the desk. "I, uh, I just thought you looked familiar is all."

He smiled. "Probably the Santa suit."

"Yeah, probably," I said.

"Have a seat."

I pulled out a chair and sat down, my shadow mimicking my every move on the back wall. For a second I watched him peck the keyboard, staring at the word TINSTAAFL on his Santa hat. Each letter was made of silver glitter and obviously hand-glued with Elmer's to the white fur. Something I'd done many times before as a kid. "So you want to tell me why you're hiding out at your own party?" he asked.

"Because my dad's got me talking with a bunch of Dilberts, that's why. He's outta control."

He laughed. "Yeah, I know how he gets sometimes. We went to high school together. He used to embarrass me too."

"Then why did you hang out with him?"

The old man looked at me with serious eyes. "Because he's a hell of a guy, that's why. He cares about people. He's just got a funny way of showing it sometimes."

He leaned back in his chair and crossed his red velvet arms. "You know, Hudson," he said, his voice warm with advice, "there aren't many people out there in this world that are gonna fight the good fight for you. Who care enough about you to tell you when you got toilet paper on your shoe or a booger in your nose. Only family does that. And when they're all gone, all you've got left are memories. Memories of what they taught you ... or memories of what might have been. And whether you know it or not ... those memories are your only legacy." He leaned forward and cocked his holiday head. "And I understand that you're sitting here feeling sorry for yourself now because you're out of a job. But you know what?"

"What?"

"False pride has killed many a proud man. So has arrogance and sarcasm. The key is to be grateful for what you've got. So while you're sitting here on your lazy butt brooding about your fate, your geeky father is out there selling you—talking you up to a bunch of strangers." He pointed a finger at me. "Something you should be doing for yourself. And if you think this is his idea of an ideal Christmas Eve, then you're wrong. I know your pop. He'd rather be out there shooting the bull about the Lakers or chasing some tail. But he's not. He's doing it because he cares about you. But more importantly, he wants you to understand."

"Understand what?"

The old man pointed at the silvery word on his hat. "TINSTAAFL." His pronunciation of the word was enough to get one hooked on phonics. The *tin* was pronounced like it read, but the *staafl* part rhymed with *waffle*.

"What's that?" I asked, a drum roll going off in my head.

"One of your father's favorite philosophies. It stands for"—and his finger traced each letter as he said it—"there is no such thing as a free lunch."

"What's that mean?"

"It means every decision you make has got a cost. To you, or someone else. Therefore, nothing is ever truly free. It also means you gotta work for everything you get out there, kid. 'Cause nobody's gonna give you squat in this world." He smiled. "Except for your dear old geeky dad out there." He looked up at the ceiling fan and chuckled, as if he'd remembered some funny story about my father in simpler times. And it was then, at that moment, when I realized what he was talking about. My father was out there doing the hard chicken on my behalf—crowing and clucking and flapping his wings all on account of me. And I gotta tell ya, it's hard enough wearing your own chicken suit out there, but wearing it for someone else is a killer.

I thought about what it would be like if my father weren't around anymore. What would I have left? Other than a bad attitude ... *nothing*, that's what.

"Anyway, kid," said the old Santa, "you think about what I said." I watched him stand up. "School's out. I have work to do."

"What kind of work?"

"I'm going to liven up this party."

"How?"

He grinned and his ashy walrus mustache flattened out into a straight line. "I'm streakin' it, son." He suddenly disrobed, the Santa suit crumpled around his ankles, and I caught a glimpse of his saggy old nudist colony butt. He strolled for the door, then stopped in the frame. He took off the hat and tossed it into my lap.

"Sweet dreams, kid."

When he dashed into the living room, I heard an explosion of laughter, then a loud scream. (Patsy Grubel, as it turned out.) Then more bursts of laughter, followed by vigorous party chatter.

Evidently, it had been a successful streak.

I sat back in my chair, smiled, and put on the TINSTAAFL hat. I felt tingly all over—a lot better about things—knowing that someone actually cared enough about me to wear a chicken suit on my behalf. The old man was right. It's all about family. What else is there?

"Is this where the cool people are hanging out?"

The voice belonged to an angel. I looked up and saw my sister standing in the doorway, her perfect white teeth exposed by a wide smile. The seven-year age difference between us really showed tonight. Although she had just turned twenty-two, she didn't look a day over seventeen. She was dressed casually in blue-jean overalls, black Converse high tops, and her arty white-blonde hair was now cut short like a boy's. She was fresh and clean and beautiful, and all I wanted to do was hug her.

"Yeah," I said, "we tend to gravitate toward the back of the bus." I stood up and we hugged. "Merry Christmas, Hill," I said, holding her tight. "I missed you."

"Merry Christmas, big bro," she said. "I missed you too."

When we pulled back, she grabbed an envelope from her pocket and handed it to me. "Brought your Christmas present."

Normally when one receives an envelope on a holiday, it contains a trite little card with a canned saying that some cleaning lady wrote on her day off. But you don't mind slogging through the drivel (common courtesy) because you know there is usually a check or a smiling Ben Franklin in there just waiting to flutter out. But this was my sister. And I knew her bank account like my own. That is, nonexistent. But aside from that, I knew that even if she did have the dough, she would never be so vulgar as to present me with cash on Christmas. That just wasn't her style. (Although under current circumstances, tonight would have been a good night for her to break with that tradition.)

"Go ahead," she said. "Open it."

Usually, at this moment in the conversation, I would've started in with the wisecracks and complaints—my targets ranging from her current boyfriend to Mr. Perfect's destiny to make my life unbearable. But I didn't feel that way anymore. And if I could've taken back all the nutty things that I'd done to her as a child while growing up, then I would have. Like the time I scolded her for wearing her first training bra. How was I to know at what age a young girl would be needing one? I was just trying to protect her from the outside world. That's all. Or the time she willingly let me conduct Chinese water torture on her. I mean, who else but a loved one would lie still on her back, fully clothed in the bathtub under the water spout, no less, while I slowly dripped water onto her forehead every two seconds? It worked. It drove her nuts. As I suspect it would anyone.

Looking back on it, and trying to put a positive spin on all of the idiotic things that I'd done to her in the name of sibling love, I couldn't help but think that I'd also done something right as a big brother. And if anybody needed proof of that, all they had to do was meet my sister. A sister who thought of the rights and feelings of others rather than her own, a sister who still believed in me.

When I opened the envelope that night, I found a card with a poem on it. It was written by Hillary. I wasn't surprised because she often gave me poems when I was down. But this poem was special. She wrote it for me.

"Well," she said. "Read it out loud." So I did.

"Dare to be great
Do not listen to those who say it cannot be done,
for they are the voices of the past.
Dare to be great.

Do not trample on the path of mediocrity,
for it is well worn with the prints of pessimism.
Dare to be great.
Do not be afraid to walk alone when
all others have abandoned you.
Dare to be great.
Do nothing but what your heart truly desires,
for it will always lead you to the truth.
Always—
Dare to be great."

I don't want to talk too much about it right now, but I got really choked up after reading that. But in a good way. I felt my body rushing with love, and all I could do was hug her. God, I thought, she was inspiring! And I remember that if it weren't for my father screaming at us from the living room, I would've hugged her all night.

"Hillary! Hudson! Get in here for the picture!"

It was Mr. Perfect calling for the annual Christmas card picture. (To be used for next year's Christmas cards, of course.)

I took off the TINSTAAFL hat and said, "How does my hair look?"

She smiled. "Pretty darn good for an unemployed dude."

"I'll leave it on," I said. I placed the Santa hat back on my head. "No use in scaring Mr. Perfect's new clients next year."

We walked toward the door, and she said, "What's the hat mean, by the way?"

"I don't really know," I said, still protecting her from the harsh realities of life. "The old naked guy gave it to me on his way out."

My belief is to leave innocence intact for as long as possible. No need to court cynicism when it seems to find you anyway.

When we spilled out into the crowded living room, the music of Frank Sinatra's "My Way" was playing loud over the stereo system. Most of the guests didn't seem to notice us because they were all too busy, shoulder-to-shoulder, cocktail glasses in hand, singing and swaying along to the Chairman of the Board's famous anthem. Mr. Perfect was busy focusing the camera on a tripod aimed at the Christmas tree. When he noticed us, he motioned with one hand.

"Okay, guys," he said. "Hurry up. The timer's going off in thirty seconds." My sister and I shared a look, and then we all huddled around the lighted tree. Hillary was in the middle. "Smile," my father said. We all smiled at the camera, and at that moment I remember glancing at the big-screen TV. *How the Grinch Stole Christmas* was on, and it was toward the end when the Grinch's heart was growing bigger in his chest. A revolution of the spirit is what it was, I remember thinking—a revolution of the heart. Something I, too, had experienced on that very same night.

When the lightbulb finally flashed, I turned and smiled at my father. He smiled back. Somehow, without words, we had agreed to communicate more. I more willing to listen, and he more willing to let me find out some things on my own. I could tell he was proud. And at that moment I felt like the luckiest man alive. If the measure of a man's success in life is determined by how many people show up for his party, then I wanted to be just like my father.

Oh, now you've got me all teary-eyed just thinking about it. So now would be a good time for me to jam—bow outta here gracefully. I don't want some critic accusing me of sentimentality and patness. (As if that were some crime against humanity.) I'm not gonna tell you what I'm doing right now, because I don't need the extra competition. But I will say this—I ain't no mortician.

Anyhow, I'm late for an appointment, and I'm tired of rambling. Keep overhead low, save some cash, always take a piss before the interview, and stay positive. And remember, pyramids always favor their architects.

Beware of any company where you gotta bring your own coffee cup—guys who call you pal on the first interview—and places where the clocks don't work. And always, always, think for yourself and read the fine print on everything. *Everything.*

That's all I can tell ya. It's rough out there. Tradition is dead. So use this story for whatever it's worth, and try to do the right thing whenever possible.

Just remember, there is no loyalty. There is no security. So don't let them tell you that there is.

It's every man for himself out there.

Or is it?

-Acknowledgements-

THE AUTHOR wishes to send out a bouquet of thank yous to Terrence and Tania Moloney for taking a genuine interest in my work all these years, for seeing a writer, not a hobbyist. (I've got watercolors for that.) To my mother, who has encouraged all of my creative pursuits, no matter how crazy. Thank you for letting me find my creative center. And to my father for his constant source of strength and inspiration, and his knowingly and unknowingly funding some of these crazy ventures. Thanks to Richard Moran for his excellent editing—for setting this novel down the right path. To the talented Kira Rubenthaler of Bookfly Design, for the final proofreading polish and making the manuscript shine. And finally, a big cantankerous thank you to my high school English teacher, Mr. Bell, who first introduced me to the concept of TINSTAAFL. I didn't know what it meant at the time, but I sure as heck do now. Thanks to all … rock on.

-About the Author-

HARLIN HAILEY was born in New Orleans and educated at the University of Southern California. Free of vampires, shapeshifters, and werewolves, he writes contemporary adult fiction set in sunny climes. Dark humor, a strong social undercurrent, and music and pop culture references often characterize his work. In another life, he has pounded the pavement for corporate America, guest DJ'd on the "World Famous" KROQ radio station, and dabbled in the exciting field of no-money-down real estate. He is the author of *East of Lincoln* and *The Downsizing of Hudson Foster.* He lives in Los Angeles.

IF YOU ENJOYED the book, please consider leaving a positive review. It is the fuel that keeps all indie authors running.

THE AUTHOR WELCOMES all comments, rants, typo sightings, suggestions, and queries from rabid fans who want the skinny on his upcoming releases. He can be reached at:

HarlinHailey@gmail.com

Made in the USA
San Bernardino, CA
08 August 2020